"We need to get out of here."

Glass broke behind her; a shot whizzed by her ear.

"Get down, Sadie," Kip said as he slid down beside her. "I'll cover you. Make a run for the back door."

"And if there's someone there?"

"Shoot to kill."

Panic ripped through her. But she couldn't leave Kip.

"On three," Kip said. "One...two...three."

Sadie sprinted for the back door. Shots rang out, but she didn't turn back. She kept running into the dark woods. Ducking and moving around the huge tree limbs. She ran till she ached, and she struggled to catch her breath.

"What am I going to do?" If Kip made it, he'd come looking for her. If he hadn't... No, she couldn't lose him.

Then she heard the crunching noise. Footsteps bearing down on her. Someone was closing in.

This was it. She was going to die.

RACHEL DYLAN

writes inspirational romantic suspense. Being a Georgia girl, she thrives on sunshine and warm summer days. She loves animals and is active in animal rescue. Rachel enjoys adding lovable pets to her stories. She lives in Atlanta with her husband and five furkids—two dogs and three cats. Rachel loves to connect with readers. You can find Rachel at www.racheldylan.com.

Out of Hiding

Rachel Dylan

HARLEQUIN® LOVE INSPIRED® SUSPENSE

Recycling programs for this product may not exist in your area.

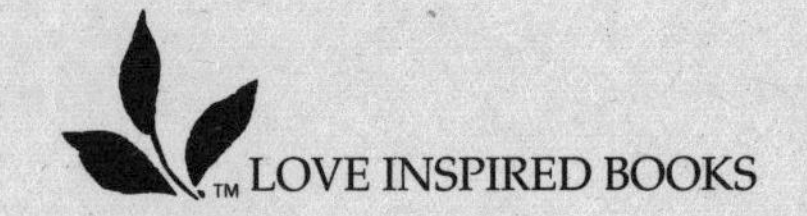

ISBN-13: 978-0-373-44616-2

OUT OF HIDING

This edition published by arrangement with Love Inspired Books.

www.Harlequin.com

Printed in U.S.A.

And we know that all things work together
for good to them that love God, to them who are
the called according to his purpose.
—*Romans* 8:28

In memory of my loving father, an amazing man of faith—pastor, teacher and friend to so many.

Thanks to my agent Sarah Younger
for believing in me and in this story.
To my editor Emily Rodmell for your keen insights.

Thanks to Alison Stone for helping me along this wonderful journey and sharing this experience with me. I cherish our friendship. To Susan Chandler for always being there and cheering me on.

To my husband, Aaron, and five furkids for your unconditional love. And to my mom who is my rock.

ONE

Sadie felt the bullet whiz by her head as she crouched down in the wet dirt. Darkness surrounded her, but she wasn't alone. Her gut screamed loudly that something was terribly wrong. And she always trusted her gut. She had company, and if that bullet was any indication, they meant business. The sound of the crackling leaves told her someone was moving quickly in her direction.

Dressed in all black, she lay flat on the ground in the dark woods. No one was going to see her. That bullet wasn't meant for her but was intended for someone else. Who? She didn't want to stick around long enough to find out. She prayed that Megan wasn't out here in the woods tonight—alone, scared and with bullets flying. It was no place for a sixteen-year-old girl.

She checked her gun and kept her position low against the damp, muddy ground. Her night vision goggles were a blessing. It was then she saw what she dreaded the most. The letters FBI on a dark-colored flak jacket as an agent trounced his way through the woods. Why the FBI was involved in whatever was happening in these woods she didn't know, but she didn't like it. They were invading her turf.

Sadie had her first solid lead on the Vladimir network in El Paso, and she didn't want to give up the opportunity. She'd been on stakeouts for weeks, desperately trying to determine if Igor—the man who had taken everything from her—was in El Paso. Her intel had been that something related to the Vladimir crew was going down in the woods tonight. She had hoped that whatever it was wasn't going to involve Megan—the missing girl she was looking for. Sadie knew that Vladimir's crew was responsible for her disappearance. That's why she'd sought out the job just days ago.

Technically, she was still in the Witness Security Program commonly known as Witness Protection, although they didn't consider her to be in immediate danger anymore. She'd followed all their rules over the years. Her new life, her new name, everything. Done by the book. Not a single deviation from the protocol given to her by the U.S. Marshals. There was no way she'd let them know what she planned to do now that she had confirmation Igor sought to set up shop in her own backyard. It was only a matter of time before Witness Protection realized Igor's activities had expanded down to El Paso, and then they'd want her to move. She needed to act fast if she had any chance of taking out Igor's network.

She slowly stood up using a large tree as a shield. Thankfully, she was small of stature. By the time she'd registered the crunch of a stick right behind her it was too late. A large hand grabbed her shoulder with another muffling her scream.

"FBI, don't move," the deep voice said directly into her ear.

Didn't matter who he was, when a man put his hands

on her, he was going to pay. She'd trained for moments like these. She slammed her foot down on his, and he groaned. But he didn't loosen his grip. Was this guy made of iron?

Trying another approach, she went limp in his arms, shocking him into loosening his grip, giving her a moment to slide away. She'd only taken two steps when he tackled her, knocking her to the ground. She could barely breathe. She squirmed against him, but she was no match for his size and strength. He had to have been at least a foot taller and a hundred pounds heavier. For a moment, fear seized her. She said a prayer asking God to keep her safe and then fought back.

"Stop struggling," he said quietly, his voice steady. "I promise I'm not going to hurt you."

She didn't believe him. She knew better than to trust the Feds. Trust them, and she could end up dead like her parents. He adjusted his grip just enough for her to knee him in the stomach. Big mistake on her part. Now he seemed raving mad.

"I'm trying to save your life here. You have no idea what you've gotten yourself into. You should not be here in these woods right now."

The thing was, she actually wasn't a stranger to life-and-death situations. So this one didn't faze her too much. "I already dodged one bullet and was doing just fine on my own."

"You'll have time later to explain how you ended up in the middle of an active FBI investigation packing heat and wearing night vision goggles. For now, let me get you out of here safe and sound."

She shuddered. Those promises had been made to

her before. And they'd been broken—every single one of them.

"I'm not going anywhere with you," she said. She struggled against his secure grip.

"Yes, you are, ma'am. Listen to me." He paused, his breathing ragged. "Things are only going to get worse. You might not be as fortunate the next time a bullet gets fired. And I don't want to have your death on my conscience. I have enough guilt to last a lifetime. So when I say three, we move for that next tree. You hear me?"

Realizing her current options were limited, she relented. He was right. Her best move for now was to retreat. She'd taken a taxi tonight and made her way to the woods on foot. It wasn't as if she had her own ride out of danger. She'd have time to get away from him once they got to safety. "Okay."

"One, two, three, go go go!" he said in a low voice. They sprinted from their current position to the next tree and squatted down. That's when she heard another round of gunfire. Automatic weapons this time. Her heartbeat quickened, but now was not the time to panic. She'd been in worse situations without the valuable experience that she now carried with her after years of being a private investigator.

"What next?" she whispered, trying to catch her breath.

"Make a run for that far tree. My Jeep is beyond it. I'm hoping that will work."

"And if not?"

"I'll think of plan B."

He sounded so sure of himself. Typical for FBI types. She wasn't going to count on him to get her out of here safely. She would survey her options once they made it to the next tree before she jumped in the Jeep of a total stranger—even if he was in the FBI. Hadn't she already learned that tough lesson?

"Now," he barked.

She ran ahead of him using her small size and speed to her advantage, making it to the tree first. Though he wasn't far behind. She saw the dark Jeep parked behind a cluster of trees providing them with additional cover.

"Let's go for it," he said.

Making a split second decision that she prayed she wouldn't regret, she slid into the passenger side and ducked down low. Before she could even steady herself, the FBI guy had turned the ignition and floored it. The bumpy ride had her on high alert as he navigated the vehicle over the rough terrain.

She stayed down not knowing if they were safe from the gunfire and started plotting her escape. No way was she being taken in by the FBI to "explain herself."

They drove a few minutes in silence as the Jeep weaved through the wooded area and onto the country road that would eventually lead back into town. Then he spoke after checking his mirrors. "We're in the clear."

She eased up into her seat and looked around at her surroundings, including the man driving. She wasn't wrong in her initial assessment. This guy was tall and bulky. She already knew from the encounter in the woods that he was strong. His brown hair was cut short. She couldn't see his eyes since they were focused on what lay ahead. She told herself to remember that he was one of them.

He glanced over at her. "You want to tell me now what you were doing out in the woods?"

"My job," she snapped. Who knows what he thought she was doing, but her answer was completely truthful.

"And what job is that?"

She sighed, already not enjoying this line of questioning. "I'm a private investigator."

"You're not plugged into our FBI investigation, though. I would've known it."

"I have no idea what investigation you're working on." She let out a deep breath and figured she needed to provide an explanation. Maybe it would help her get away from him sooner. "I was in the woods searching for a missing girl. You may have even seen a local news story about her. Her mother recently hired me. I've been looking everywhere. I didn't see or hear anything until I felt the first bullet whiz by my ear." She was telling the truth. She had to make sure Megan wasn't in those woods tonight. It appeared that her leads had been correct. Something was going on with the Vladimir crew. And the FBI was involved. She said another silent prayer for Megan.

"Wow," he said. "You were in the wrong place at the wrong time, Ms. P.I. lady. I'm going to need to bring you in, though. Gotta take your statement. Make it official." His Southern drawl was unmistakable.

"I don't think that's a good idea."

"I promise it'll be quick. You are carrying a weapon. I assume you have a permit for that and all."

No way she'd allow him to take her in, but she didn't have to tell him that. Her past struggles with the FBI were her own. Better to have the element of surprise.

"Uh-oh," he said. He jerked the wheel hard to the right sending her into his right arm. "We've got company. Hold on."

"I thought you said we were good."

"They came out of nowhere."

She turned around and saw a large dark SUV that was gaining on them. But FBI guy had some moves and was taking the curves on the dark country road with finesse as he drove toward the more populated area of town.

"Who are these people?" she asked as she clenched her fists. Were they connected to Vladimir?

"The less you know the better."

"Why don't you let me take a shot? I could probably blow out their tire."

"You're that good of a shot?" he asked with disbelief dripping from his deep voice.

"You better believe it," she said without hesitation.

He paused for a second and glanced over at her. "If you think you can, then go for it."

She was going to show this FBI guy that she was no slouch. In fact, she could probably outshoot him. All the time she'd spent at the range over the past few years had paid off. She turned around and was glad they were in a Jeep. Granted it didn't provide them with much, if any, protection, but it also meant she'd have an easier time getting off an unobstructed shot.

Steadying herself she took a deep breath, aimed and pulled the trigger. It only took one shot, and the right front tire of the car chasing them was done for. The pursuit ended abruptly as they began to skid, the car circling in on the blown tire. "Got 'em."

"Well, Ms. P.I. lady, I'm impressed."

"You should be." Then she turned the gun toward him.

"Whoa." He lifted up his right hand at her while keeping his left on the wheel. "Just put that thing away."

Her hand was steady. “I have no reason to use this on you. But I’m not being taken in for questioning. I didn’t do anything wrong.”

“I never accused you of anything,” he said with a raised voice. She watched as his hands tightened on the wheel.

“Take me downtown. Let me out and drive away. It’s that simple.”

“You’re crazy, ma’am.”

“No. But I’m the one with the gun right now, so I hope you don’t try anything crazy.”

“You’re hiding something.”

“It’s none of your concern. Just act like you never saw me tonight.”

“You know that’s not possible. I’ll have to write up this whole thing.”

“Be creative,” she countered. “Now let’s get downtown. And don’t try anything because I’d really hate to shoot you.”

He let out a deep breath but started driving toward town as she directed. *Good,* she thought. She doubted that he’d let her go indefinitely. But she needed to get away and deal with this problem on her own terms. That meant not being taken in for questioning by the FBI tonight. She needed time.

When they reached the more crowded streets of downtown El Paso, she was ready to get away from him. “Slow down. Let me out. And keep on driving. Do you hear me?”

“Yes,” he said in an even voice.

“Good.”

He did as she asked and slowed down. She never took the gun off of him as she opened the door slowly.

With the light from the streets flooding in, she could see his eyes were light blue. And questioning. "Just pretend I was never here. For your own good and mine too, okay?"

She couldn't shake the thought that she'd seen him before. She backed out of the Jeep, and he didn't say anything in response. She slammed the door shut, and he pulled away. She didn't waste any time weaving her way through the Saturday night crowd.

She was safe for now, but she had no doubt. The FBI guy would find her, and when he did, she'd be in a ton of trouble.

Kip Moore had a job to do. He actually had several. In addition to bringing down the branch of the Vladimir network that had popped up in Texas, he had to find the infuriating P.I. who had the nerve to draw a gun on him.

He didn't know whether to be impressed or insulted. She might have been small, but someone had taught her how to shoot—and to shoot well. There were only so many P.I.'s in El Paso, so tracking her down wasn't difficult. His P.I. lady was in truth, Sadie Lane of The Lane Group.

He needed to figure out her connection to the Vladimir network and his investigation. He was going to offer to bring her in as a consultant on the case. It would be the perfect way to find out what she was up to. He was currently on his way to pay her a visit. Turned out her office was on the outskirts of downtown not too far from where he'd let her out on Saturday night. It was part of a larger row of nondescript offices, and he read the sign outside her door confirming he was in the right place.

He was prepared for just about anything when he walked through the door, but he wasn't expecting to stare down the barrel of her gun yet again. He couldn't help but smile. "We can't keep meeting like this."

"Didn't I tell you to leave me alone?"

"Yes, ma'am, you did. But it wasn't very polite of you to draw your gun on me the other night after I helped get you out of that mess in the woods."

"I told you I wasn't planning on using it. And I was more than capable of getting out of 'that mess' as you call it, all on my own. If you haven't noticed, I'm pretty good with my gun."

He laughed and looked at her closely. In broad daylight, she was even prettier than he'd noticed Saturday night. She wore dark jeans and a simple navy T-shirt. Her long brown hair hung loose down past her shoulders. Unlike so many women, she didn't have makeup caked on her face. That was a plus. But it wasn't like he had any time to date. Even more so, he didn't have any business dating. Not right now, maybe not ever again. He quickly pushed those thoughts away.

"Why don't you just lower the gun so we can talk without threats?"

"And why would I do that? You'd have yours pulled on me in less than a second."

"You are a smart lady, Ms. Lane."

She raised her eyebrow at him, and her dark chocolate eyes narrowed in disapproval.

"I'm Special Agent Kip Moore with the FBI. You can just call me Kip."

"Agent Moore," she said, as she held her head high. "I have work to do. I don't have time for baseless FBI inquiries right now."

"I'm sorry, Ms. Lane, but if you don't talk to me now, I'm going to come back and hound you every day until you do."

She scrunched up her nose, and he could tell that she was thinking of how to play things.

"What do you want from me?" she asked.

"Answers."

"I told you on Saturday night why I was there. I was searching for a missing teenager named Megan Milton. I don't see that there could be anything else for us to discuss."

"We didn't find evidence of any missing teenager in the woods."

"I went on a lead. You have to understand that when a child is missing, every lead must be checked out."

He was skeptical but was letting it go for now. She was holding back on him. "All right. I can understand that."

"Good, so now we're done."

He put up his hands. "Not so fast. Could you please lower your weapon now? I promise I won't draw mine on you. You have my word."

Her lips turned up into a smile and amusement flashed through her eyes. "I don't even know you, Agent Moore."

"I'm a federal agent."

The room fell silent. After a few moments, she looked him directly in the eyes. "I would be a fool to take your word on anything."

She was frustrating. Even more so because she had a point. "Okay, can I at least have a seat while I talk?"

She nodded. "That's fine."

He took a seat across from her desk in a comfortable chair, and took a moment to gather his thoughts. "First, things first. Here's my FBI identification." He removed his credentials from his pocket and slid them across the table. She picked up the ID with her left hand, still holding the gun in her right. After studying it for a minute, she nodded.

What was the best way to get through to her? "I need to know what you saw in the woods Saturday night. Take me through it step by step."

She opened her mouth to speak, but he lifted his hand. "And before you say you didn't see anything, remember that I know you had on night vision goggles. Looked like military grade if you ask me. And since I was in the military, ma'am, I'm quite familiar with how they work. So I know you could see and that you saw something."

She sighed. "Could I see, yes. Did I see anything? No. I heard a lot of noises, but I never got visual on anything other than some FBI guys. And then you."

He nodded. Was she telling him everything? "Why don't you let me buy you lunch and see if anything more comes back to you?"

"It won't," she responded quickly.

Too quickly. Maybe he needed to provide her with an incentive to get involved. "I'd like to be able to tell you more about the investigation in hopes that you could assist us."

"Assist the FBI?" she asked.

"Yes, ma'am."

She did that scrunching thing with her nose again and didn't seem to be too enthused. Maybe he'd made the wrong move. He'd thought she'd be intrigued by the prospect of working with the FBI, but it seemed now that was not the case.

"I'll have to pass." She visibly relaxed and set the gun in front of her on the desk.

"Even if it involves working on a high profile case? Taking down some Russian mob types from New York that have shown up in El Paso?"

He watched as her eyes widened and the color drained from her face. Then she tipped over in her chair. He was by her side in a few steps. The woman had passed out on him. He really had his hands full now.

"Sadie, are you okay?" a deep voice asked. She must be dreaming. Igor's grimy face flashed through her mind—his ice-cold blue eyes mocking her. Igor could find her. Hunt her down. He was close. So close. She was in danger. She felt strong arms propping her up. She knew the voice from somewhere but couldn't place it. Then at that moment it came rushing back to her. Her eyes popped open, and her heartbeat raced. She tried to reach for her gun.

"It's okay, it's Kip. Sadie, you with me? Have you eaten today?"

She couldn't process this. She'd been camped out for two weeks waiting to get a glimpse of Igor coming out of the five-star downtown hotel, but she'd never seen him. Her worst fear, confirmed. The Vladimir network was expanding to El Paso. And the FBI was on the trail. She couldn't let this Kip guy know the truth. She knew Igor could be in El Paso, but hearing the words brought about a visceral reaction within her.

"Sorry. I haven't eaten. Sometimes I get a little queasy, low blood sugar and all." She was hypoglycemic, but her reaction was spurred by something much more sinister.

He reached into his jacket pocket and pulled out a protein bar. “Here, eat this.” His light blue eyes flashed with concern.

“Thanks,” she muttered. This was it. She wasn’t safe here any longer. She’d been tracking Vladimir’s network closely, well, as close as possible, but hadn’t been sure Igor was in the area. Parts of his crew, but not Igor himself. She had known all about his continued operations in New York. The human-trafficking ring that spread up to Canada. As she suspected, his next move had to be expanding into Mexico. But now she had to focus, she had to pull herself together, and quickly. She took a couple of bites of the protein bar as Kip sat silently watching her eat.

“You feeling any better?” he asked.

“Yeah. Where were we?” She needed more information from him to determine whether her initial research was accurate. And while she’d never trust the FBI after what they let happen to her family, she needed Kip’s knowledge right now.

“I was saying that we could use your help in the investigation involving a Russian crime syndicate. It’s actually a family business of sorts that started in New York. They’ve sprung up a satellite office down here, so to speak. Human trafficking over the border.”

“And where do I come into this?” She wanted to close her eyes and pray that there was no way he knew about her past with the Vladimir family. He couldn’t. That person no longer existed.

“I saw you in action on Saturday. You’re good. I also

think you know more than you're letting on. So I was hoping you could consult on the investigation with us."

"You don't even know me."

"I've seen enough. And of course, I had the FBI run a background check on you."

Thankfully, her history before joining Witness Protection was in a sealed file that wouldn't even show up on his search. Add on to that the additional Witness Protection security protocols. But still she wouldn't put anything past the FBI. Igor Vladimir may have pulled the trigger and killed both her parents, but it was the FBI's fault that he had been in her house in the first place.

"So what do you propose?"

"Lunch." He smiled.

"Not happening," she said. She wanted more information, but she needed to do it her way.

"Coffee?"

"Possibly. I wasn't lying. It's Monday morning. I've been busy catching up on things with more ground to cover. We can set something up for later today if you're really serious."

"I am. And I can work with your schedule."

"Meet me back here at two," she said. That would give her enough time to do some digging.

"All right." He turned and walked to the door, then looked over his shoulder. "Please don't draw the gun on me again." He winked and stepped outside.

She needed to drink some water and clear her head. The room felt like it was closing in on her. Her panic attacks had gotten better, but at times like these they threatened to claim her again. She couldn't believe she'd passed out earlier. That was dangerous. Super dangerous. She knew the information she'd been given about Igor was probably true, but hearing it out of Kip's mouth had still been a shock. She was smart enough to know this Kip Moore wasn't one of the FBI agents responsible for her parents' death, but the fact he was still a part of the Bureau made her uneasy.

She laughed to herself. Work with the FBI? Really? She despised the FBI's bureaucratic maze for failing her parents, and rightfully so. However, it would seem that she needed to work with them now to get what she ultimately wanted. Justice. She'd been working toward this goal for years on her own. Going against the shadowy Vladimir network in any small way she could. This, though, could provide her an opportunity to deal them a huge blow. Her two greatest enemies. Could she work with one to take down the other?

TWO

Sadie worked furiously updating her research on the Vladimir network. The FBI had more resources than her. But they'd both been in the woods Saturday night, so they weren't too far ahead. What was the FBI going to be able to do anyway? The same old thing, which in the end meant nothing.

She felt the pressure building around her temples. Her phone rang loudly, and she shook her head trying to focus.

"The Lane Group, this is Sadie," she answered.

"Sadie," a woman's voice said. "It's Carrie Milton. Have you found out anything more about Megan? It's been over a week now since she's been missing."

"Hi, Ms. Milton." Sadie dreaded telling her that basically the only news she had was no news. "I followed up on a potential lead over the weekend. But unfortunately it didn't go anywhere."

Ms. Milton sniffed. "I'm just so worried about her. The police aren't taking this seriously enough. It doesn't seem like they're totally focused on this."

"Nothing's ever going to be enough until we find her. I've talked to the local PD. They are looking for her, but it's always better to have more options. From what you've told me, Megan is a very smart girl. I'm going to do everything in my power to find her."

"I wasn't meaning to imply that you weren't doing your job. I know you've only been on the case a few days. I just can't describe to you what it's like to know your child is in danger. But that's not the main reason I called. Megan's best friend, Lauren, wants to talk to you. She thinks she might be able to help. They are very close."

"Send me her contact information, and I'll get in touch with her right away."

"Thank you so much, Sadie. Now, we haven't got around to talking about your rates yet. I don't have a lot of money. I work two jobs as it is. But I'm willing to do whatever I need to do to help find her. Maybe we can work out some sort of a payment plan?"

Sadie's heart ripped in two. "Don't you worry about that right now, okay? I'm sure we can work something out within your budget. I've already started investigating, and I'm not going to stop. In the meantime, I'll need you to send me some additional pictures of your daughter and Lauren's info."

"I can't thank you enough."

Sadie provided Ms. Milton with her email address for the pictures, and she jotted down Lauren's contact info. Ms. Milton promised to send pictures right away, as soon as they discontinued their call.

The bell on her door jingled, and Kip was standing there with his arms crossed. She looked forward to the day when she could have a more sophisticated entry with a receptionist. It must already be two o'clock. Ugh, he was the last thing she needed to deal with right now.

"Glad to see you're not armed." He took a few steps toward her.

"I don't have much time to chat. I just talked to the mother of the missing child I told you about. I have to do more to find her."

"Shouldn't the police be taking the lead on that?"

"The mother isn't satisfied with the police's effort. Can you blame her? It's her child."

His eyes softened. "I understand."

"Let's make this quick."

"No coffee?"

"I can make some here if you'd like?"

He smiled. "That'd be great."

She loved coffee. It was one of her biggest weaknesses. Sadie was glad he wanted some too; she liked being able to brew a pot for more than just herself.

Her office wasn't large, but she had what she needed. She dreamed of expanding and having another investigator and eventually an assistant. Maybe one day. Then it would really be The Lane Group; for now it was just her and her trusty coffeemaker. She started the coffee and then took a seat back at her desk. While she had told him she wanted to make it quick, what she wanted was more information. With Megan's disappearance, her personal goals might have to wait.

"I just want to make sure you didn't see anything more on Saturday night? No matter how small, I want to know everything."

"I can walk you through it. Again. I was there, in position. When I felt the bullet literally graze by me. I could hear noises but couldn't see anyone. In fact, the only people I saw were in FBI flak jackets—two of them. And then there was you, of course."

He gave her a crooked grin. "Yes, then there was me. And you left out the part about holding me at gunpoint."

She couldn't help but laugh. "I didn't think you needed to relive that, right?"

"Seriously, though. This Vladimir group is bad news. They're involved in a bit of everything, but the most egregious part of their operation is human trafficking. I'm guessing I don't need to tell you what that all entails. They also have a full drug and money-laundering scheme. And they run a variety of legal businesses that help serve as cover."

"So why the move from New York?"

"Easy. The Mexican border. They move these poor girls over the border, and then…I can't tell you how awful these men are."

He didn't have to. She knew. "And I could help how, exactly?"

"You've already shown you're a good shot. Plus you're a P.I. I'm sure you have expertise that could help out the FBI investigation."

She nodded.

"But mainly, you probably have your ear to the ground with sources we don't have at the FBI. If you hear anything, see anything in your work, we'd appreciate knowing about it. As you can imagine trying to take down an operation like theirs is a huge job. And we still may not succeed. They've eluded us before. This isn't a simple takedown. It's a very complex operation."

She thought for a moment then asked. "How long have you been in the FBI?"

"Three years."

"That's it?"

"Yeah, before that I was in the military."

"What branch?"

"Army."

"You weren't just the in army though, were you?" she asked on a hunch.

"Ranger."

"I could tell.

"And how is that?"

"You have an edge about you."

"I guess I should take that as a compliment?" he asked with a raised eyebrow.

"Yeah, I think so."

"So what do you say?"

"If I have any information, I'm happy to share. But right now my top priority is my client and trying to find this missing girl."

"What do the police say?"

"That they're overstretched on resources but still doing everything they can. No leads though."

"Are you concerned?"

"After talking to her mother, yes I am. Moms know best. If she believes something happened to her daughter, then who am I to question that? The girl's friends also haven't heard from her. That's key. A teenager might ignore her mom but definitely not her friends."

He frowned. "Doesn't sound good. How old is she?"

"Sixteen."

"When did she go missing?"

"Saturday before last while out downtown with her friend."

He frowned even deeper this time.

"What?" she asked.

"Nothing." He shook his head.

She knew that wasn't really what he was thinking, but she'd let it go.

"I know you're busy. So I'll get out of here. I'd like to take you to lunch sometime, though."

"I'll think about it."

"Good." He stood up and walked out the door.

She couldn't help but notice how sweet his smile had been. Or his concern over Megan. Army ranger. Those guys were no joke. Why did he have to join the FBI? She shook her head in disgust. The FBI had a way of messing everything up. She hoped Kip hadn't been corrupted. She shouldn't focus too much on his sweet smile. Megan Milton was her top priority.

Sadie didn't waste any time getting to work after Kip left her office. She needed to talk to Lauren and retrace Megan's steps from the prior Saturday night. She'd gotten the teenager's address from Ms. Milton and arrived at the house out in the El Paso suburbs. Lauren's family had money. The two-story white sprawling house with a perfect fence was so cliché.

She'd called ahead of time to confirm the meeting. Lauren and her mother were actually eager to talk to her. She rang the doorbell and was greeted by a woman with bleached blond hair, in her forties, dressed in a tennis outfit. However, her perfume and heavy makeup didn't seem consistent with an intense tennis match.

"You must be the private investigator?"

"Yes, I'm Sadie Lane. You must be Mrs. Newton."

"Yes. Please come in. I'm so glad you're here." She waved her hand in the air. "Lauren has been absolutely distraught. She won't even go out which is so unlike her. She's a social butterfly. I hope you can help. She's anxious to talk to you."

"Before I talk to her, how well did you know Megan?"

"She spent a lot of time over here." She shook her head. "She's a sweet girl." She lowered her voice. "But her mother." She leaned in closer. "She actually works two jobs."

Sadie tried to reserve judgment, but Lauren's mother seemed pretty judgmental herself. Sadie admired the fact that Ms. Milton worked two jobs to support her family. Obviously, from the looks of the expansive house, Mrs. Newton didn't have to worry about money.

Mrs. Newton fluffed her already-teased hair. "At any rate, her mother leaves Megan alone a lot. It's sad, but Lauren's taken her under her wing. My Lauren has her act together. Top grades and a blooming social life to go with it." She held her head high. "I'm so proud of her. She's the perfect daughter."

Sadie wanted to laugh. This lady probably had no clue what her daughter was getting into. "That's wonderful that Lauren is doing so well, and I'm glad she's a friend to Megan."

"Yes, I'm sure she'll want to talk to you now." She called out to her daughter, and Lauren bounded down the steps. She was a younger version of Mrs. Newton. Her much more natural blond ponytail was perfectly styled, and she also wore a buff-pink tennis outfit. Maybe a mother-daughter tennis match this evening after the summer sun subsided?

"Lauren, dear, this is Ms. Lane. She's the investigator looking for Megan."

"I'm glad you're here," Lauren said. She walked right

over to her and grabbed Sadie's hand dragging her into the living room. "Mom, can you give us a few minutes to talk?"

"Sure, dear." Mrs. Newton bounced out of the room, oblivious.

Lauren plopped down on the couch and leaned her head back for a moment before turning and making eye contact with Sadie. Sadie sat down beside her.

"I'm freaked out about Megan," Lauren said bluntly.

"I'm so glad you're talking to me. I'm going to need you to be completely honest with me. No one is in this room right now but me and you. To be able to help Megan I need to know the whole truth."

Lauren nodded. "I get it." Lauren tightened her ponytail, and then looked directly at her, her blue eyes wide. "That's exactly why I asked Mom to leave. She can be so controlling and always wants to add her spin to any story."

"Start at the beginning. What happened that Saturday night?"

"We were going out downtown for a nice dinner. We scored the top two grades in our AP history class. Megan had been saving up for months for this dinner. Megan's family doesn't have money. It's just her and her mom, so this was a big deal. Once we got the grades, we immediately started planning."

"Okay, so what happened?"

"We made a reservation at the newest and trendiest restaurant in town. I couldn't believe we were able to get a reservation, but we did. It's the one inside the fancy Rhubarb Hotel called Sala. It's also exciting because they play live music, and it's just the place to go. So anyway, we were at our table and there was a delay in our getting served because it was so busy. I went to find our server to get us some water. By the time I got back, she was gone." Tears welled up in her eyes, and she looked away. "If I hadn't left her, maybe she'd be okay."

"How long were you gone?"

"The restaurant was packed. It was probably at least fifteen minutes or longer. Because—" she paused, looking down "—I took a detour and wandered around a bit, taking it all in."

"So the last time you saw her, she was at the table. Then fifteen minutes later or longer you walked back, and she wasn't there. Then what did you do?"

"I looked for her. I checked the ladies' room and the hostess stand. Then went back to the main seating area. Sala isn't that large. After I went around the place at least three times, I knew something was wrong. Megan and I like to go out and have fun, but we never ever leave each other like that. She would not have left that restaurant without me. No way. We know it's not safe. Something happened to her." Her eyes misted up. "I know it."

"What did you do then?"

"I went home. Megan's mom was working the night shift. So I didn't talk to her until I called the next morning. She hadn't seen or heard from Megan either. That's when I flipped out."

"And you never got any word from her? A text, an email, anything after that night?"

"Nothing." She paused and her blue eyes filled with tears yet again. "What do you think happened?"

"I don't know. But I'll do my best to find her."

"I know I'm just sixteen, but I'm not stupid. Could someone have taken her?"

"That's always possible."

Lauren stood up and started pacing. "I'm so mad at the police. They need to be doing more. I've watched enough TV to know that this isn't exactly a top priority for them. They aren't taking this seriously enough. They don't want to commit more resources. It's not right! I think if my family hadn't gotten involved they wouldn't be doing as much as they are now."

"That's sad," Sadie said in truth.

"I know."

"If Megan was in trouble, is there anywhere she would go?"

"Yeah. She'd come here. To me. To my house. Megan has been through a lot. Her mom works so hard. Megan even got a part-time job at the yogurt shop when she turned sixteen. And her dad, he's never been in the picture. Like ever." She hesitated and shifted her eyes away again. "I don't know what I'll do if something happened to her. I may put on a big act that I'm all put together, but Megan is the strong one."

"You've been very helpful, Lauren. Is there anything else I should know?"

"I'll do anything to help, Sadie. Anything."

Sadie said her goodbyes to Lauren and her mother and went back to the office, settling in at her desk. A few minutes later, she looked up as Kip walked through her office door smiling.

"What're you doing here? I told you I was working this case."

"I wanted to see how your afternoon was going. Any leads on the girl?"

"Maybe. I went to see her friend. What do you know about Sala?"

"The swanky restaurant in the Rhubarb Hotel?"

"Yeah."

"I'm not into the fancy restaurant scene."

"Me neither."

"But I've heard it's the trendy place to go in town. They have live music on the weekends which is a big draw for the college crowd. During the week it caters to business types and young professionals."

"I'm going to have to go there tonight."

He frowned. "Why?"

"That's where Megan was last seen. I need to ask around about her. Someone there saw something. I just know it."

"What did the friend say?"

"She left Megan at the table alone while she went to track down their server and look around the place. When she came back Megan was gone. She looked everywhere and couldn't find her."

"I'm coming with you."

"I don't need an escort to a fancy restaurant."

He laughed. "Believe me, you've made it clear you can take care of yourself. But I can do my own recon while we're there."

"For what?"

"See if I can get any tips on the Vladimir operation."

"You think you'd get that at Sala?"

"The newest report from the field team is that Igor has been seen going in and out of the hotel. It's his speed. Plus, Igor is in the hotel business—the high-end hotels anyway. He also has a few five-star restaurants."

At the sound of Igor's name, chills shot down her arms. "Igor?" she asked.

"Yeah. The Vladimir group is headed by the father, Sergei. But his two sons, Igor and Artur, actually do the work. They're currently in a battle for who's going to take over."

"Interesting," she said. "So Igor is here in El Paso?"

"He comes and goes, as does Artur. But Igor has staked out El Paso as his territory. He appears to be putting down roots."

"You asked me a lot of questions about what happened in the woods, but you never told me what went down that night."

He ran his hand through his dark hair. "We tailed one of Igor's thugs who was involved in a money drop into the woods. Looked like there was some hand off there between the thug and some other guy who we're still trying to identify. Most likely linked to the trafficking business. Makes me sick."

"What do you mean?"

"The guy was probably making a payment for more girls."

She shuddered to think about it. "You're trying to stop Igor's network."

"Me and my team."

"So they take the girls over the border, then what?"

"You really don't want to know."

He was right. She didn't need the gory details. She understood exactly what happened to those poor girls. "All right. Well, I need to go home and shower before I go out tonight."

"What do you say about grabbing dinner before we

go to the hotel? I'm in the mood for Italian. We can discuss some operational details."

She considered rejecting his offer immediately but then thought better of it. This man was the key to tracking down Igor. "That would be fine. Why don't we meet somewhere for dinner?"

He shook his head. "No, I'll pick you up."

"You don't even know where I live." Then she realized he was in the FBI so he could easily track her down.

"I'll find you. How does seven-thirty work?"

"See you then."

He smiled and walked away. She hoped she wasn't making a big mistake.

When Kip pulled up to Sadie's little house, he stopped for a minute to gather his thoughts before exiting his FBI-issued sedan. What exactly was he doing here? Yeah, he didn't want her going to that fancy downtown restaurant alone, but why should he care so much? He'd cared once before and look where that had gotten him. A broken heart. No, not just a broken heart. His ex-fiancée, Lacy, had ripped his heart out and stomped on it.

Her having cheated on him was hurtful, but the fact that she'd left him for Brad Sullivan—one of the guys from his own ranger team—nearly killed him. Brad had been not only his friend but also someone he'd looked up to as a military leader. They'd bonded after a team retreat in Brad's cabin in Colorado that they'd taken before they deployed. The pain was still fresh even though it was now years past. He'd never be able to forgive. Ever.

This was business, though. If the FBI report was correct, Igor might be using the hotel as his base of operations. He took a deep breath and stepped out of his car. He knocked lightly, and the door opened. The sight of Sadie took his breath away.

"Hey," he said.

"Come on in. I just need to feed my cats."

She was simply stunning. Her long straight dark hair flowed over her shoulders. She'd changed into a pair of black slacks and wore a dark green shirt that looked amazing against her skin. It was made out of some kind of silky material that seemed soft and feminine. He looked at her again as she poured cat food into a dish. Her smile was enough to make his heart unsteady.

Two cats came flying into the room meowing loudly. One was black and the other orange.

"Meet Leo and Sammie."

He slowly stepped closer to them, and they looked at him skeptically before turning to the food dish.

"They friendly?" he asked.

She laughed loudly. "Depends on what they think your intentions are."

"I'm an animal lover. Really a dog person, but cats are okay, too."

"Do you have a dog?"

"Yeah. A yellow Lab named Colby. He loves everyone."

"I like dogs, too. Pretty much all animals. But these kitties are perfect for my lifestyle." She smiled again. "I'm ready if you are."

By the time they reached the restaurant, he had admitted to himself that he wished this was a first date. He had no idea what Sadie thought. She was tough to read. He'd picked a casual Italian restaurant that he loved named Primo. They had the best homemade pasta in the city.

He hadn't wanted to freak her out, but on the way to the restaurant he thought they'd picked up a tail. He was going to keep his eyes open.

"Hope this is okay?" he asked.

"It's perfect. I'm addicted to pasta of all kinds."

A hostess guided them to a corner table, and he chose the seat against the wall facing the restaurant so he'd have the best vantage point of the room. If there were any threats, he'd be able to identify them.

The smell of the sauce had him realizing how hungry he was. He'd only had a power bar for lunch. The restaurant was busy most of the time, and tonight was no exception. There was just enough noise and people for it not to seem awkward between them.

He smiled at her. A server walked over immediately to take their drink orders. He ordered water, and she ordered an unsweetened tea.

"So tell me a bit more about you, Sadie."

The server popped back over with their drinks and warm bread. Sadie diverted her eyes for just a brief second, looking down at the menu, and then glanced up making eye contact again.

"I grew up in Oregon. Then went to college here in Texas at UT. And I've been in El Paso ever since graduation."

"Where are your parents?"

Her eyes shifted again. "They're still in Oregon. Mom's a teacher, and dad's an architect. I'm very close to them even though I don't visit enough. I try to talk to them on the phone often. What about you?"

"I moved a lot. Dad was in the army. So we were all over the place, but I spent a good chunk of time growing up in the South. I went to The Citadel, and then joined the army." He took a big bite of the buttery breadstick.

"How long were you in the military?"

"Until three years ago. Being a ranger got to be a bit too difficult after a while." That was an understatement. "So I retired and joined the FBI."

"Why the FBI?"

"Law enforcement was a good fit. I thought I could use everything I'd learned as a ranger and really make a difference."

She cocked her head to the side. "And are you?"

"Am I what?"

"Making a difference?"

"I'd like to think so."

The server came back, and they both ordered pasta. He opted for spaghetti to satisfy his craving, and she surprised him with her choice of fettuccine Alfredo—the richest pasta on the menu.

"And why are you a P.I.?"

"I also wanted to make a difference. But I like being my own boss. I didn't want the constraints of a system that allows important details to get lost."

Interesting, he thought. He wondered what caused her to distrust government agencies. She didn't have to say it, but he knew there was a more complex story brewing under the surface.

"Who taught you how to shoot?"

"A friend I met in college."

Ah. He was curious if this guy was a lot more than a friend to her. But it wasn't his place to pry right now.

Their meal came, and he was glad she didn't pick at

her food but ate eagerly. They both finished off all their pasta, and he even dove into a second basket of breadsticks. But now dinner was over, and it was time to get to work. Thankfully, he hadn't identified any threats in the restaurant.

"So do you have a plan for tonight?" he asked.

"Scope it out. Talk to some people. Show her picture to a few of the workers. You know the drill. What about you?"

"See what I can see. Make sure not to make waves. More watching than talking if you know what I mean. I'd love to actually confirm for myself that Igor has been hanging out there." He reached over and picked up the check.

"Let's split it," she said.

"No." He smiled. "This one's on the FBI." He opened his wallet and pulled out some cash.

"Are you sure?" She frowned slightly.

"Absolutely."

"Thank you."

"Let's do it."

Once they got in the car, she looked over at him. "That was a nice dinner, Kip. But when were you planning to inform me about the tail we picked up on the way over?"

THREE

Sadie tried to push back her anger. Yeah, she'd just called him out. He didn't realize that she wasn't some amateur P.I. She'd probably noticed the tail before he did. Sadie was used to being underestimated.

He let out a sigh. "I didn't want to worry you."

"You should've told me. If you want to work together you can't keep information like that from me."

"Understood."

"You think it's connected to the work you're doing on the Vladimir case?"

"Probably. Or myriad other things. As an FBI agent, I have my fair share of troubles."

She grinned. "I feel the same way about being a P.I. But honestly I can't imagine doing anything else."

Sadie's heartbeat sped up as she and Kip got closer to the five-star Rhubarb Hotel. They parked in the public lot a few blocks down since they didn't want to park at the hotel or use the valet service. The warm summer night air made it difficult to catch her breath. She felt entirely out of place at such a fancy hotel, but for her job she had to adapt.

Kip didn't look like an FBI agent tonight. He would

blend in well in the crowd with his black slacks and stylish light purple button-down. Given the nature of his undercover work, she still hadn't seen him in the typical FBI suit. His short brown hair was neatly styled.

Kip had made at least two calls back to the El Paso field office, but he'd taken them in private, leaving her wondering what exactly they'd talked about. She had to be patient, or he'd question why she had so much interest in Igor. There could be a link between Megan's disappearance and Igor's operation. That's why she needed Kip's help and the FBI's information on Igor.

It bothered her that she hadn't been able to be fully truthful with Kip at dinner. But she couldn't be with anyone. Under the rules of Witness Protection, she had to keep up her cover for the rest of her life. Unless the threat was neutralized completely.

"You ready for this?" Kip asked, breaking her out of her thoughts.

She took in a deep breath. "Yeah."

They walked into the main entrance of the hotel, and the opulent chandeliers took Sadie's breath away. Lush maroon couches and huge upholstered chairs filled the lobby. The Rhubarb was the nicest hotel in town. It housed two restaurants. A formal dining restaurant and Sala, which was still very nice but more trendy. The live music was a big draw on the weekends. They stepped into the lobby and took the elevators up to the second floor where Sala was located. Once they got to Sala's entrance, Sadie noticed that it wasn't that crowded, but there was still a good number of people even for a Monday night.

She had a job to do. "I'm going to go to the hostess stand and see if I can find someone to talk to."

"Okay," Kip said. "I'm going to grab a table in the casual lounge area. Keep an eye out on things."

She nodded and walked over to the hostess stand. A young woman stood there along with a man wearing a manager tag. He was probably in his forties, and his dark hair was smoothed down. He didn't look like he'd be one to be messed with even in his formal restaurant attire.

"Do you have a reservation?" the young woman asked.

"Actually," she said looking at the manager. "Can I have a minute of your time?"

"Sure," he said. "Please, let's talk over here." He motioned to the expansive waiting area.

She pulled out a picture of Megan and Lauren and showed it to him. "Have you seen this girl on the left?"

"Who's asking?"

She smiled. Hoping to get more information by being nice than being aggressive. "This girl has been missing since Saturday before last. I'm trying to locate her."

"And who are you?" he asked with raised eyebrow.

"I'm a P.I. hired by her mom. And I just want to find this girl. Please."

"I do remember her—both of them were here. I thought they were a little young to be eating here alone, but they said they were celebrating something for school which I thought was very nice. This girl," he pointed to Lauren, "was a bit too flashily dressed for her age in my opinion. But the girl you are looking for looked quite appropriate for the evening."

Sadie sighed. "I know that a lot of college kids come here on the weekends, too. Have you had any problems here with guys trolling the place, any date rape drug issues?"

He shook his head vigorously. "No, no. Nothing like that. Not here at Sala. We have security, and we are a five-star restaurant at a five-star hotel. Our reputation can't allow something like that to happen. But that stuff happens all the time, though, at Sapphire down the street. We're not a club, but a restaurant. A very nice restaurant. We close at midnight even on the weekends. Most of the college kids come here for the live music, but then go out after that. We're the first stop of the night. And the ones with money will have dinner during the performances."

Hmm. She wondered. "Can you remember anything else?"

"I'm sorry I can't help you more. I saw her here, but I don't remember seeing her with anyone specific. Her friend was up near the stage hanging on some guys, though."

Ah, Lauren had neglected to mention that. What else had she left out? "Is there anyone else here you think I should talk to?"

"Most of the college crowd from the weekends aren't very observant. And tonight's mostly regulars. Business dinners, fancy dates, stuff like that."

"What about the staff? Hotel security?"

"We'll cooperate in any way possible. But I'm guessing you won't get very many details. This place is packed on Saturday nights."

"Thanks for your time," she said.

"I hope you find her."

She sighed and walked over to find Kip sitting at a small table in the lounge area.

"Anything?" he asked.

She shook her head. "He thinks she was here, but that's about all he can say."

A tall man brushed her shoulder as he walked toward the bar and whistled at the bartender. She looked to her left, and her heart almost stopped. Paralyzed with fear she couldn't breathe. The man turned back and looked directly at her but showed no sign of recognition on his face. He was not just any man. He was Igor Vladimir, otherwise known as the man who murdered her parents and destroyed her life.

"Larry, send me a bottle of champagne to my VIP table all right? I'd like it with my steak." He didn't wait for an answer and walked away.

Kip leaned in and whispered in her ear. "That's Igor."

He didn't have to tell her that. She'd know that man anywhere. Granted it had been years since she'd seen him, but she could never forget. He hadn't recognized her at all. The last time she'd seen him in person was almost twenty years ago. She'd grown up. Changed. But she was still scarred by the memories that his presence brought to the surface. She felt a panic attack coming on. She needed to get out of there.

"I need some air." She didn't wait for a response before standing up from her chair and walking quickly to the exit. Deep breaths, she told herself. The world was closing in on her again. *Please, Lord. Make it stop.* It felt like someone was squeezing the breath out of her.

Then Kip's hand landed on her shoulder. "Sadie, are you all right?"

She nodded her head but kept walking.

"What's wrong?"

"Was getting a bit crowded in there." She gasped for air and avoided directly answering his question.

He cocked his head to the side, clearly trying to figure out what was going on with her. "I know getting close to a man like Igor is difficult, but he doesn't know us. We're safe."

"Don't worry about that. I'm fine, really." Or she would be. She needed a plan.

"It's getting late. Why don't I take you home?"

"Megan's still out there. I need to do more."

"I know. But you're not going to find her tonight, Sadie."

The way he said her name, warmed her heart. Like he actually cared about her. She knew better than to believe that, though. She couldn't trust this FBI guy. Even if he seemed nice. Hadn't Martin seemed nice too? Just the thought of him made her nauseated. He hadn't done his job, and two innocent people were dead because of it.

"Sadie, you with me?"

"Yeah, sorry. You're right. Just take me home." She needed some time to think. About everything.

Kip wondered what had happened to Sadie last night. She'd been fine, and then she'd lost it. Kinda like when she fainted when he was in her office. Maybe it wasn't just her blood sugar. Maybe she was prone to panic attacks? If so, what were her triggers? There was a lot more to Sadie that he didn't know, and to his surprise, he wanted to learn more.

He leashed up Colby and got ready for their morning run. They never missed a day. It was therapeutic for Kip. And the Labrador loved to run. Colby was his best friend. He understood him. His dog was loyal and loving. Unlike his so-called friends who had abandoned him in his time of need. They had sided with Brad in Iraq. Even worse, they'd supported Brad when he stole away his fiancée. His teammates all made excuses for Brad saying it was the way things were meant to be. In Kip's book, cheating was never meant to be. And stealing another man's fiancée was an absolute breach of trust.

What a disaster his life was, well, had been. He was finally starting to get things back together. However he couldn't let his own personal issues get in the way of his job. There was too much on the line now. He was the team leader on this mission, and it was up to him to come up with something concrete. A way to get to Igor and bring down this operation once and for all.

Colby started running faster, and Kip loved the feeling of freedom he felt jogging with his dog. Then it hit him. What if he was able to infiltrate Igor's El Paso network? He'd done more difficult things as a ranger. It wouldn't be easy, but if he could pull it off then it would be worth it. Now he just had to figure out how in the world to go about it. He questioned his initial interpretation of Sadie being in the woods that night. Yeah, she may have been doing some surveillance, but he felt almost certain she wasn't involved with Igor's operations.

He finished the run and wondered what Sadie was up to today. Probably trying to track down her missing teenager. He didn't like the circumstances surrounding the missing teen. He hadn't wanted to say anything to Sadie last night, but in the back of his mind he couldn't help but wonder if Megan had been taken by Igor's operation. He had a nagging feeling about it and was going to get one of his guys to do some digging.

The fact that he now knew Igor had a VIP table at Sala made him believe Igor might be running some of his business through there. A five-star hotel that housed a fancy restaurant popular with the younger crowd on the weekends was the perfect way to prey on innocent teenage and college girls.

Men like Igor deserved much more punishment than the legal system could give them. He didn't do a lot of thinking about God lately. It was too difficult not to remember how God had forsaken him in his time of need after Brad's betrayal. But he hoped God found the right punishment for Igor.

Sadie had to get a grip. She couldn't let Igor intimidate her. The way she'd acted last night was unacceptable. She needed to gain control of her emotions fast, or he would win. Like always. She needed a list. Her top priority still had to be finding Megan. She was disheartened by what she'd learned last night, or rather what she hadn't learned. She felt more strongly than ever after seeing Igor that he had something to do with Megan's disappearance.

When she'd gotten the initial reports that Igor had moved his operations to Texas and that he might be involved in human trafficking, she knew things were going to get complicated. Then she'd heard about Megan's case on the local news and had prayed there wouldn't be a connection between the two. But knowing it was a possibility, she'd sought Megan's mother and offered her services.

Kidnapping young girls was the perfect way to add to a human-trafficking ring. What if Igor had taken Megan? She closed her eyes and prayed that it wasn't the case. Prayed for Megan. Prayed for Megan's mom. And Lauren. And finally she prayed for strength for herself. She needed guidance from God. Her faith had only grown stronger over the years. Her biological parents had not been people of faith. But her adoptive parents had been. They'd taken her to church. Taught her strong values and to trust God. They were a constant steadying force in her life. She wanted to thank them every day. Because without Him, she would've never lived to be twenty-seven. She didn't even know Lydia Mars anymore. She'd been Sadie Lane for the past nineteen years. Lydia was dead. She'd died the day Igor walked into her house and shot her parents in cold blood.

The FBI had claimed they were safe. She'd overheard conversations that even an eight-year-old could understand. And now she understood even more. She'd found out a little more over the years from her Witness Protection contacts. However, it was painfully clear the FBI had dropped the ball. They'd waited too long to call in the U.S. Marshals and put her family in Witness Protection. So long that Sadie had been the only one left to protect. What had her father gotten into that caused Igor to kill him? That question still haunted her. For now, though, she had something else she had to focus on. Another child's life hung in the balance. There was nothing she could do for Lydia, but there was a lot she could do for Megan.

When her office door opened, she instantly knew it would be Kip. He walked in looking handsome as ever—his blue eyes twinkling. She didn't want to think he was attractive. Deep down he was still the enemy. But when he smiled at her, her heart felt light. A feeling she wasn't accustomed to. She desperately wished she knew what he was thinking.

"What's going on?" she asked.

He walked over and stood in front of her desk. "I know you're busy looking for Megan. But I have an idea to run by you."

"Okay." What was he up to?

"I'm going to try to infiltrate Igor's network, and I need your help."

She felt her eyes widen. "What? Have you lost your mind? You really think an active FBI agent can get into Igor's network?"

"Just hear me out. I have a plan."

Stay calm, she told herself. "All right."

"You and I would team up. Present Igor with an offer he couldn't refuse."

"Which is?"

He took a step closer to her. "A dirty FBI agent."

She sucked in a breath. This was too much.

"Sadie?"

She tried to focus. "A dirty FBI agent. How?"

"That's where you come in. I need a partner. A partner on the dark side who lured me into this business. For money, of course. I think it's a more believable story if I have a woman who I'm motivated to act for."

"This seems insane."

"I know." He sat down in the office chair and ran his hand through his hair. "But I think it could work. I obviously have FBI support and contacts, so we could make it convincing. I just need you to be the mastermind behind it all. I'll play the pawn to your queen."

She took a deep breath, trying to calm down. "And you think he'd believe all of that. To what end?"

"The deal would go like this. I'd tell him he's the target of an FBI investigation. I'd provide him valuable information. For a great price."

"And who exactly am I?"

"A devious and demanding lady. We met when I tried to arrest you on a money-laundering charge connected to your drug-running operations. But you convinced me otherwise."

She didn't understand where he was going with all of this.

"Don't you see? It makes it more likely that something or someone would cause an FBI agent to go astray. You're that for me. A P.I. with a mind of her own and an interest in side businesses. Very lucrative and illegal side businesses."

"I don't even know what to say."

"There's something else."

What else was he about to lay on her?

"I'm worried Megan could've been taken by Igor's guys."

Her pulse quickened. "I had the same concern, especially when I saw him at the hotel."

"Unfortunately, it's more than just a hunch. I just got a call on the way over here from one of the guys on my team. They've been doing some recon and noticed Igor's guys leaving with various young women—from that hotel. Everything points to Igor setting up shop there. He's definitely staying in the penthouse. He may not be responsible for Megan's disappearance, but I still think there's a good chance he is. So if we could get inside, maybe we'd have a chance to find her."

"Maybe." He was right. But she shuddered. With more time, would Igor ever recognize her? She didn't think so. Nineteen years…from a child to a full grown woman. He'd never know what hit him.

"So what do you think?"

Without thinking through any of the implications, she made an impulsive decision. "I'll do it."

He sighed. "You know this is dangerous."

"I'm aware of that."

He nodded.

"When do we start?"

"Tonight. I just have to okay everything with my superiors, but I think we should go back to Sala and orchestrate a chat with Igor."

"Great," she said. What she actually meant was, *I'm gonna be sick.*

He reached out over the desk and grabbed her hand. "We can do this."

He felt warm, and she really wanted to believe they could do this. She also really wanted to believe in him.

They returned to Sala, and the first thing Kip asked Sadie to do was find the manager. He wanted her to make sure the manager was willing to keep his mouth shut about the conversation she'd had with him. Kip had worked his sources and there was no evidence tying the manager to Igor in any way. Then he'd had a colleague at the FBI run a background check on the manager which also came up clean, so he felt it was a good strategy to keep the manager looped in.

Kip hung back, and she walked over to the bar and talked for a few minutes. Then he heard her loud laugh. It was infectious. Man, she was infectious. She couldn't have been more different than Lacy. Lacy was tall, very thin and very blonde. He thought Lacy had a heart of gold, but he'd been wrong about that. He still held Brad the most responsible.

He studied Sadie. She was short, with long thick dark hair and eyes so dark he found himself drowning in them more times than not. She had secrets though. He could tell. But could he really judge? Didn't he have enough of his own?

Sadie reached over and patted the manager's hand. Then she slowly walked over to Kip, her eyes checking out the entire restaurant.

"So?" he asked.

"It went well. I think we're fine. He doesn't want to do anything to jeopardize finding a missing child. I didn't get the sense he was one of Igor's men."

"Good. We don't need any complications."

"You can say that again." She kept scanning the room.

"He's not here yet."

She nodded.

"I've got a table in the corner reserved. Will put us close to what I've been told is his usual table."

"Let's go then."

"I'm ordering some appetizers. We don't want to stick out."

"That's a good idea."

They settled in at their table and waited. And waited some more. Finally, almost an hour later, he saw her eyes light up. Then he followed her line of sight. There he was.

"He's here," she whispered. "How're we going to play this?"

"You need to approach him."

"Me?" she croaked.

"Yeah. It's the only way. He'll be way too suspicious if I do it."

He watched as she clenched her fists, but her face was unreadable. "You okay with that?"

"I can do this," she said.

"You don't have to convince me. If I didn't think you could do it, I never would've asked you to."

She nodded.

"And you're a woman. You'll have a much easier time getting an audience with him."

She laughed. "Yeah, the last time I checked I was female."

He felt stupid. Why did she cause him not to be able to be as articulate as usual? "It's time."

"I got this."

Oh, she didn't have anything. She might be putting on a brave face for Kip, but she was scared to death. Her biggest concern was being recognized by Igor. Flashbacks hit her hard. On the witness stand. The defense attorney grilling her, trying to poke holes in her story, verbally destroying her. And she had only been a child. She almost hated that attorney as much as Igor. She had been telling the truth. Yet, no one believed her. They saw her as a scared child, not as a reliable witness to a double homicide. The jury had acquitted Igor, and now here she stood about to face him nineteen years later. She wanted justice. Or revenge. There was a fine line between the two that she'd been treading for years. She prayed that she wouldn't let this consume her. She didn't want to be filled with hate. But for Igor, that's all she had. She couldn't help it.

Now was her chance, though. She might not ever get

another opportunity like this. She said a quick prayer asking for more strength. She'd have to be convincing. This performance needed to be compelling. Because if it wasn't, she might just get herself killed. Then who would help Megan? She had to succeed.

She stood up and walked down to his table. He was talking to a few women in fancy dresses who surrounded him—obviously trying to make a play with them.

"Why, hello," he said. His eyes were as menacingly icy blue as she remembered. "Take a seat and join the fun."

"I'd like to talk to you in private. About business." She needed to be tough. Ruthless. Convincing.

"Ah, well, tonight I'm not working. You can call my people and make an appointment." He slipped his business card to her.

"No, actually, I can't. I'm here with a onetime business proposition. I doubt you'd want me to start discussing it here in front of all your new friends." She eyed the women at the table.

He narrowed his eyebrows at her, and for a split second she thought she had been recognized. Then he cocked his head to the side. "All right. Ladies, please give me a minute. I've got some pressing business matters I must attend to."

The women grumbled and stood up from the table. Sadie took a seat across from Igor.

"So, you have five minutes. I don't like my pleasure time to be interrupted, Ms.?"

"Lane."

"Okay, your time has started."

"I'm a P.I."

"Is that so?"

She clearly had his interest piqued. "Yes. And I have a friend. Someone I met because of my other business interests."

"And who is this friend of yours?"

"An FBI agent."

"If you're messing with me, Ms. Lane, I can assure you, you'll regret it."

"No. I'm not. My friend has come to realize the FBI is not the job for him. I convinced him to work with me instead of against me. Since then we've teamed up on various business ventures that utilize his vast resources and pad his wallet. In exchange, I get access to FBI information. Now I would like to share something with you if you'll let me continue."

"Why should I do that?"

"I know something you'd want to know."

The icy look returned to his eyes. She was going to be able to do this. One step at a time. "But I want something in return."

He raised an eyebrow. "You're really trying my patience here."

"The FBI is investigating your El Paso operations."

That got his attention. His eyes widened and then he quickly recovered and laughed. "I'm sure I'm constantly investigated by the Feds for one thing or another. Why is this any different?"

"This is more serious. The entire Vladimir network is at risk."

He leaned forward. "And you're telling me this why?"

"Because I want my friend to serve as a conduit of information. You'd know what the FBI knows. You'd be a step ahead of their game. Of course, this would all come at a price. A big price."

He didn't say anything. But she could tell by the frown on his face that he was concerned. And he was considering what she said carefully. His blond hair was a bit shorter than when he was younger. And he had aged quickly. Probably from all the booze and drugs. But he still looked menacing. She had to try to stop the chill that threatened to overtake her.

"You're playing with fire, Ms. Lane."

"I usually do." She smiled. God give her strength to keep this up.

"Where is this FBI friend of yours?"

"He's at that table over there. The really big guy." She nodded in Kip's direction.

"I need to think about your proposition. Why don't I give you a call if I want to discuss this further?"

"No," she said quickly.

"No?" He looked incredulous at her response. No one defied Igor.

"Like I said, this is a onetime offer. I'm above all things a shrewd business woman. I don't have time for games. I'll move on to my next opportunity if you aren't interested."

He reached across the table and grabbed her wrist hard, but she was ready and countered him by quickly removing his hand. "Don't touch me," she said in a frigidly polite manner.

He leaned back in his chair and laughed. "You know, you're growing on me. So refreshing to see a woman with an actual backbone. You should forget this FBI goon and come work with me. I have plenty to offer you that he doesn't."

"That FBI goon is going to save your operations here if you're smart and accept my offer."

"Bring him over here, then. I'd like to talk to him."

"Sure." She got up from her chair, walked back to Kip and let out a deep breath. She'd done her part, now it was time for Kip to bring it home.

She stood at Kip's table. "Your turn."

He nodded. "How did it go?"

"Well. It's all you now. Don't mess this up."

"I don't intend to."

She sure hoped he knew what he was doing. She guided him over to Igor's table.

"Mr. Vladimir. This is Kip Moore."

Kip nodded at him and took a seat. Sadie sat down beside him.

"I already told Ms. Lane. I don't intend to be strung along."

Kip crossed his arms. "What I bring you is invaluable. However, there is a price on every tip I send your way."

"And if I say I don't need you?"

"Then it will be your fault when your group goes down in flames. I'll simply move on to the next opportunity."

Igor laughed. "You Fed types are all the same. So self-assured. I've been at this a long time, Kip. I'm not going to start being worried now about a little FBI investigation."

"You should be. Because they're closing in on you. Fast."

"And why should I believe a thing you say?"

"That's up to you, of course. But you'll see that I bring a lot to the table."

"You definitely bring a lot in your friend Ms. Lane."

Kip's eyes darkened. "Ms. Lane is not what we're discussing." The implication clear. Kip was staking out his turf and setting up the storyline just as they'd planned.

"Ah, I see. It's more than a business partnership between the two of you." Igor shook his head. "That's too bad."

"Why don't we get back to talking about the deal," Sadie chimed in.

"What's the offer?" Igor asked.

"I will feed you real-time intelligence," Kip said. "For a price."

"And what if your intelligence, as you call it, is bad?"

"It won't be."

"There's that arrogance again." Igor leaned forward. "Why don't we say this? Let's do a trial run. Bring me something, name your price and we'll go from there."

"I'll be in touch soon."

"Great. Now let me get back to entertaining. All this talk of business is giving me a headache." He paused, and then looked at her. "Ms. Lane, you're welcome to stay."

"Thanks, but I've got work to do." She smiled at him. It made her sick to do so, but she needed to be believable. She needed him as close as possible, so she could take him down. That's exactly what she planned to do.

FOUR

"So what's next?" Sadie asked Kip.

The two sat at the small table in her office drinking coffee.

"Last night was a good start. But now we need to give Igor a piece of intel that he will appreciate."

"We're no closer to finding Megan. That's still my top priority." She paused and looked at him. "I want to bring down this awful network, but Megan needs me to do my job."

"So do many other girls and women, Sadie. If we can get to the source, just think of the lives that will be spared. Igor is truly a monster, and we both think Megan could have been taken by those working for the Vladimir network"

"What else do you know about him and this family power struggle you described?" She wanted to get as much additional information from Kip as she could.

"The father, Sergei, is really getting too old to actively run all of their operations. He's turning more into a figurehead. Both Igor and his brother Artur want to take over." Kip paused and took a sip of coffee. "Igor is the oldest and argues that the business is rightfully his."

"What does Artur say about that?"

"That the best man for the job should take over. So the word on the street is that Sergei told his sons that he wanted to evaluate them, and then he'd make his decision. Probably by the end of the year."

"So there's a big incentive for them to perform."

"Exactly."

"Igor has his human-trafficking operation. What else?"

"He also has legitimate businesses—in hotels and restaurants. I think he may be looking to buy out the Rhubarb Hotel."

"What about Artur?"

"Artur has some casinos, dry-cleaning operations. Oh, and he runs the drug business for the Vladimir network in the Northeast."

"Doesn't that sound great," she said sarcastically.

She watched him as he looked at her neck. She looked down and saw her cross necklace was on the outside of her blouse. She touched it.

"Are you a religious person?" he asked.

"I don't really like the word religious, but I'm a Christian if that's what you're asking." The cross was a gift from her adoptive parents, and she never took it off. "What about you?"

He sighed and ran his hand through his dark hair. "I am, Sadie. But I feel like sometimes God doesn't like me so much."

She reached out and grasped his hand. "Don't say that, Kip. We all go through rough patches. For me, my faith is the only thing that has kept me going more times than I could count."

His eyes darkened, and then he looked away.

"There's a lot of time to think about God and faith out in the desert."

"When you were deployed?"

"Yeah. I did multiple tours in Iraq."

"War is awful," she said.

"I know. Sometimes it's necessary, but knowing that doesn't make it any easier."

"I would think having those experiences, and coming home, would have only strengthened your faith."

"It's complicated," he let out a deep breath. "Why don't we get back to Igor?"

"All right." She'd let it go for now. But she knew there was something deeper going on with Kip. "What are you going to tell Igor?"

"I'll make him think that I'm giving him something of value. Of course it won't be. We'll tell him about an FBI surveillance operation that's going to occur. So when it happens, he'll believe we're legit."

"And what about the actual surveillance operation?"

"Only a select group of FBI agents will know that it is for show. The rest of the team will believe it's an actual assignment. It's just surveillance, though. The risk of something going wrong is very low. Igor will get spooked that he's being followed so closely, and we'll get the buy-in we need from him. Or at least that's how I'm hoping this plays out."

"We gain a little bit of his trust and then what?"

He grinned and cocked his head to the side. "Let me ask you this. When you do your regular work do you always have things planned out step by step?"

"I'd like to, but that's not usually the case."

"It's the same way here. We go with what we have.

And what we have is another reason to visit Igor at the Rhubarb Hotel tonight."

"Tonight?"

"Yes. Is that going to be a problem for you?"

"No. I just didn't realize we'd see him again so soon." Her pulse sped up just thinking about another encounter with that man.

"I'm not going to let that creep hurt you, Sadie. I promise you."

Was she that obvious? She'd have to work more at keeping her feelings about Igor under wraps. Kip's strong presence couldn't be ignored. It didn't matter that he'd been out of the rangers for three years. He hadn't stopped training. But beyond his physical size, he gave off a vibe of confidence and strength that impressed her. While she was confident in her own ability to protect herself, it sure couldn't hurt to have him by her side.

"He gave me his number. Why don't we just call him?" she asked. She pulled his business card of her bag and flipped it over showing Igor's private cell. "I think the less face time we have with him the better. Less room for error."

Kip looked down as if trying to process her comments and didn't respond immediately. "You may have a point. But, on the other hand, we want him to feel like he knows us. Like he can trust us."

She sighed. And hoped she could get through this. Her office phone rang, and she answered it.

"Sadie, it's Ms. Milton."

Her voice was cracking, and Sadie instantly knew something was wrong. Her heart dropped.

"What's going on?"

"I heard from Megan. Just for a minute. Somehow she got to a phone." Muffled sobs came through the phone.

Sadie switched to speaker so Kip could hear.

"Slow down, Ms. Milton. I heard you say that Megan called you. Tell me exactly what you remember her saying."

"That she had been kidnapped. She spoke really quiet and said she couldn't talk for long. None of the other girls who tried to use the phone had reached anyone yet and most of them were from a group foster home outside the city. She heard the guys who were keeping them captive talking about the Mexican police and how they'd crossed the border undetected." She paused. "They were all scared of what was going to happen to them."

All of Sadie's greatest fears for Megan were playing out. "When did this call happen?"

"Just a few minutes ago. The caller ID said restricted call, but I answered it anyway hoping it was you with information about Megan." She hesitated. "You're the first person I contacted. Even before the police. I'm calling them next. I just don't know what to do. I was so thankful, so relieved to hear my baby's voice. But then when she told me where she thought she was and what was happening. I've never been so terrified, or felt so completely helpless."

"You need to call the police, Ms. Milton. But you did the right thing by calling me. I doubt they can trace the call if the number was blocked and you only spoke for a few minutes, but you still need to contact them. Megan was very smart to have the presence of mind to call you. You need to have faith that we'll be able to find her. You have my word that I will do everything in my power to locate her and bring her back safely. The best thing you can do is stay calm. And if you hear from her again, please let me know. Any detail no matter how small can help us. Ask her about what she hears, the smells, anything."

"Mexico is a huge country! How can you expect to find her without more? And what if it's too late?" Ms. Milton's voice shook. "What if they ship my baby off to another country? I know what this is all about, Ms. Lane. I'm not naive. Her life is literally on the line here."

"I understand the gravity of the situation. Please believe me. I've got a few ideas of where to start searching. Now call the police and tell them what you told me. And if you think of anything else or need me at all, just call me." Her heart broke for Ms. Milton. While she was telling her to stay calm, Sadie knew that if she was in Ms. Milton's position she'd be a complete wreck.

She hung up the phone and Kip stared at her, frowning. "What?" she asked.

"They moved quickly, not wasting any time in crossing the border. Now that they're in Mexico it will be quite a challenge. I was hoping that we could've intercepted them before they crossed."

"I wonder how Megan got to a phone?"

"Sounds like she's a smart teenager. It's good she has that going for her. But I hope she doesn't get too bold. That's the easiest way to get herself killed. You know they wouldn't think twice about that."

A cold shiver shot down her arm because she knew what he was saying was right. "We can't worry about how she got the phone right now. I need to get to Mexico, ASAP." She stood up.

"Wait, wait." Kip walked over quickly and gently

grasped her by her shoulders looking her straight in the eyes. "You can't just run down to Mexico. We need a better understanding of the situation. The best way to get that is through Igor. We have to stick to the plan."

"Time is running out. You know that they won't keep those girls as a group in Mexico that long. We may not have time to get more intel," she implored.

His strong hand was still resting on her shoulder, and when he dropped it away, she missed the steadying touch.

He let out a deep breath. "I hear you. Let's compromise. Give me a little time to work on Igor and to contact my other sources. That's all I ask."

She thought about all he said, knowing that wandering aimlessly around Mexico wasn't going to work. They were racing the clock. With each second that passed, the risk of never finding Megan again increased. She had some ideas about where they could be in Mexico—at least cities for starters. But that wasn't enough to go on, she did need more information.

"Fine, we'll do it your way, but 'a little time' is just that, okay? You have until tomorrow morning, and then I'm going it alone. They can't be too far into Mexico. They wouldn't have wanted to put the group of them on a plane. So they were most likely traveling in vans. They're probably not too far over the border."

"That makes sense. But Megan's call changes things. I want to go ahead and contact Igor. You with me?"

"Yes." She nodded. She needed his help. "I need you to use some of your FBI resources."

"I'm on it. Believe me this isn't my first assignment." He playfully tapped her arm.

She couldn't help but laugh. Kip was a charming guy.

She wondered why he was still single. She would've expected a good man like him to have been taken a long time ago. Besides being incredibly handsome, he was obviously smart and had a great job. Most women didn't share her disdain for FBI agents even if they might be concerned about the dangerous nature of the job.

"We'll get through this," he said. "I'm going to do the call on Speaker. But don't pipe up unless I signal you. I want to see how he's going to try to play it."

Her heartbeat sped up, and her stomach clenched. She wasn't looking forward to hearing Igor's ominous voice again. But she realized they needed to make this call. She'd do anything and everything in her power to try to find Megan.

"Hello," Igor said, his voice deep.

"This is your friend. We met last night at Sala. I promised you some information."

"Ah. Very good." He paused. "Should we discuss this on the phone or in person?"

"I think the phone should suffice for now. You've got company. They're following you."

"And what are they looking for?"

"Anything they can use against you."

Sadie realized she was holding her breath as she listened to the conversation play out. She needed to breathe.

"I need more specifics. Your vague comments are beginning to test my nerves."

"They're interested in your new business venture."

"What do you know about that?" Igor demanded with a raised voice.

"I know enough to tell you unequivocally that you should be worried about it. I also wanted to offer my services if I could be of any assistance in your operation on this matter."

"Really?"

"Yes. I hear you may need help in Mexico."

Igor cursed loudly, and Sadie drew in a breath. She hoped and prayed that Kip wasn't pushing him too hard. They couldn't afford to have this backfire on them. She had to trust Kip right now, though. *Dear Lord, please guide him to saying the right thing to be able to save the innocent lives involved.*

The silence was deafening. It felt like an eternity had passed.

"I could use your help. But only on a trial basis."

"Good," Kip said keeping his voice devoid of emotion.

"On one condition. I want Ms. Lane to be involved."

"I can arrange that."

"Let's discuss further details in person. Not at Sala though. In the other restaurant at the Rhubarb. I have a private room I can reserve there. Be there at seven tonight. Sharp. And make sure Ms. Lane is with you."

Sadie heard the dial tone. She thanked God that the call was over. She looked down and saw her fists were clenched. She could only keep praying.

Kip tried to play it cool, but on the inside his heart raced. The call with Igor had gone as well as it possibly could given the circumstances, but dangerous times were still ahead. He hated that he had to bring Sadie deeper into all of this, but he feared if he cut her off she'd be much more at risk on her own. Sadie would not give up the search for Megan regardless of what Kip advised her to do. Keeping her close was his best option. In the process though, he had to guard her from Igor and his hired guns.

He looked over at Sadie. The color had drained from her beautiful face. He couldn't help but think there was something more that he was missing. Had she dealt with men like Igor before? Did she know what they were really capable of? He feared that the answer was yes. Would she open up to him one day? He hoped so. But that was something he had no business in wanting. He was good. Just him and Colby. He'd given up on human relationships three years ago.

"How do you think it went?" he asked.

"Better than I expected. I didn't think you'd bring up the Mexico angle so quickly."

"Hey, I told you that I just needed a little time."

She smiled, and his heart melted just a little. His heart felt like an iceberg though. There was a lot more to chip away before he could open up. He needed to snap out of it and focus on the mission.

"So I guess we're meeting with him this evening."

"Yes, and hopefully we'll get the information we need to start tracking down Megan in Mexico."

"And how do you expect to get Igor to tell you anything?"

"We give him something he wants—he'll give us something in return."

"But you already gave him the surveillance report."

"That was just to whet his appetite. He'll have a lot more questions. Believe me. Men like Igor get paranoid. We're going to capitalize on his paranoia. Nothing like adding a little fuel to a sibling rivalry fire."

Her eyes widened. "You're going to throw his brother Artur into the mix."

He nodded. "Exactly. We'll plant the seed in his head that Artur is in cahoots with the FBI."

"Anything that will help us get to Megan. What will I need to do?"

"Igor has taken a liking to you. That's why he wants you there. But you need to be tough. You can't let him see any weakness, or he will jump on it. Can you do that?"

She took a deep breath. "Yes. Yes, I can. I know I've been a little off my game. But don't worry about me. I can totally handle this." She held her head up high.

"That's more like it. I wondered when the woman who pulled the gun on me was going to be back." He chuckled. "We should go by your place so you can pack. I have a feeling we might be hitting the road right after our meeting. So bring whatever you think you'll need for the trip. But don't pack too heavily. Then we can swing by my place, and I can take Colby to my buddy's house."

She nodded. "Seems like you have it all figured out."

"At least we have a plan of action."

"You seem like the type of guy to like plans. Probably from your military background. I like plans, too."

"Let's get going. It's going to be a long day."

By the time the two of them had done everything they needed to do to get ready for a possible trip to Mexico, it was nearing time for them to meet with Igor. Sadie had a sick feeling deep in her gut. *You can do this*, she kept telling herself. She was a strong, independent private investigator. She wasn't going to let this man who had taken so much from her hurt more people now. She had to do everything she could to stop him. Taking a quick moment for herself, she prayed. Not only for herself, but for Kip. And of course she prayed for Megan and the other girls. She knew she should also pray for Igor, but she couldn't bring herself to at the moment. She prayed for strength that one day she could.

"What's on your mind?" Kip asked her as they drove to the Rhubarb Hotel.

"Honestly? I was praying."

"You do that a lot?"

"Yes. What about you?"

"It's not something I like talking about." He hesitated for a moment. "I used to. I just didn't feel like He was listening. It's a long story."

"You'll have to tell me sometime."

"For now, let's focus on this meeting. Let me take the lead."

He was a take charge kind of guy. Normally that would annoy her, but with Igor she appreciated a bit of the buffer. Could she face that man alone again? She didn't know.

She looked at Kip as he scowled. His eyes were locked on the rearview mirror.

"What's wrong?"

"Someone's been following us."

"One of Igor's guys?"

"I don't know. But I don't like it. Hold on tight."

He sped up, and she braced against the seat. After she steadied herself, she turned around and saw the truck behind them was gaining. "He's getting closer. Why would Igor send someone after us now? That doesn't make any sense."

"No clue." Kip made a sudden left turn throwing her off balance, and her right shoulder hit the door hard.

"Are you okay?" he asked with his eyes still on the road.

"Yes." Her arm was throbbing and her pulse racing. The truck was gaining on them. With a thud she was thrown forward in the seat. Thankfully the seat belt prevented her from hitting her head on the dash. She sat in shock, not fully registering that the truck had just rammed them.

"Kip, you've got to step on it. He's going to hit us again." Panic started to take over.

"I'm trying. He's got a bigger and faster truck."

Before she could speak, her body jerked forward as the truck made impact a second time. Hard. Her teeth clanked together, and she bit down on her tongue. She tasted blood.

"Is he trying to scare us or kill us?" she asked with a strained voice. She was trying to stay calm, but she feared the next hit from the truck was going to be even more substantial.

"I don't know what his endgame is. Hold tight again."

Kip floored it and took a sharp turn, barely missing the cars that were speeding by. The truck had to wait to make the turn because of oncoming traffic.

She realized she was holding her breath, and then forced herself to breathe. "Where are we going?"

"We're still going to the meeting with Igor. Just taking a different route."

He handled the car like a professional race car driver. With each move that he made, she felt more confident in his skills.

By the time they reached the hotel, she felt sure that they'd lost the tail.

"That was a bit much," she said, taking a deep breath.

"If Igor wanted to send a message, he could've done it in person."

"Which makes me think it was someone else."

"Any theories?"

"Perhaps someone else in Igor's network doesn't trust us. Or wanted us to miss the meeting."

"That's possible. We were focusing on Artur earlier, but I'm sure a lot of Igor's men don't appreciate us butting our heads in. Especially if we provide intel that they couldn't bring to Igor themselves."

"We're here now. That's what matters. However, we're going to have to be more careful when we leave."

The hair on her arms stood up. She felt like someone was watching her as she entered the main lobby entrance of the hotel. She surveyed the faces around her and didn't see anything suspicious. Forget Igor's paranoia, her own was setting in at an alarming rate. Her shoulder started to ache from the impact. She hoped the night wasn't going to get worse.

"Remember the plan," he said under his breath. He gently took her arm and guided her through the lobby and down a long corridor which led to the hotel's other restaurant.

They walked up to the host stand, and her pulse pounded rapidly.

"We're here to see Mr. Vladimir."

"Ah, you must be Mr. Moore. Mr. Vladimir asks that you meet him up in the penthouse instead of down here. He was delayed working on some other matters."

"Thank you," Kip said.

They walked out of the restaurant and toward the elevators.

"How do you feel about this?" she asked.

"Not good. Don't give up your weapon. I don't care if they tell you to. Stand your ground. He likes you. But I can't help but feel like this may be a trap."

"Wait. Let's think about this for a minute." She grabbed his arm. "I'll go in. You stay behind."

"No." He shook his head. "Absolutely not."

"You said it yourself. He likes me." She paused realizing her hand was still on his biceps. She let go. "That way if something goes wrong you'll be able to help. If we both go in, it's too risky. And we have a better chance of success if I go. Alone."

He shifted his weight from side to side and rubbed his chin. She could tell she had him.

"You know I'm right." She stood with her hand on her hip. Her confidence grew by the second. This was the right call. She was sure of it.

"How long do you need in there?"

"If I'm not out in half an hour, come and get me."

"No. That's too long."

"No. I think I can do it under that, but I don't want to be worried about time. Thirty minutes. That's the deal."

"And don't give up your gun."

"I get it. Like you, this isn't my first day on the job."

She was going to face down her nemesis—get the information they needed—and save those girls.

"Be careful." He gave her hand a squeeze.

"Thanks." She smiled at him grateful for the warm look in his crystal blue eyes. She was ready. An amazing sense of calm washed over her, and the only explanation was that it was from God. She pushed the up button on the elevator watching it light up.

When the elevator arrived, she pushed the floor for the penthouse. She'd never been in a penthouse before.

Not even close. The only thing she had in her mind was what she saw in the movies. As she rode up the fifteen floors, she said another prayer. When the sound indicated she was at her destination, she settled her shoulders and took a final deep breath.

She stepped off the elevator into an ornate hallway decorated in rich hues where an ominous looking man stood on a fancy rug in front of a large double door. He was well over six feet tall with a bald tattooed head and piercing green eyes.

She walked over to him with her shoulders back and full of confidence—at least on the outside. "I'm here to see Mr. Vladimir." She figured she needed to be as formal as possible.

"Are you Ms. Lane?" he asked with an arched eyebrow, his huge arms crossed against his chest. He towered over her and probably weighed two and a half times what she did.

"Yes." She refused to let him think she was intimidated by his size.

"Are you alone?"

"I am."

"Turn around. Hands on the wall." His voice was deep and authoritative.

She wasn't going to flinch. He would get fired if he didn't frisk every person that came into Igor's penthouse. As he ran her hands roughly over her, she once again reminded herself why she was there. She couldn't let Megan down.

"I've got a gun," she said calmly.

"Hand it over."

"Not gonna happen."

"Yes, it is. I'll ask Mr. Vladimir if you can have it

back when you leave. But no way are you going in there armed. Even if he did invite you."

She relented. Kip wouldn't be happy, but she didn't have much of a choice. The thug was right. These guys had a way they operated. They didn't deviate from security protocol. And letting an armed woman into Igor's penthouse just wasn't going to happen. She pulled out her gun and gave it to the brooding muscle man.

He nodded and opened the door. She exhaled when she stepped foot into the room. It was unlike anything she'd ever seen. The foyer opened up into a large living room. A sparkling crystal chandelier hung over her head. A huge wraparound ivory plush couch was centered in the room surrounded by multiple chairs and a grand piano sat in the corner. The room prominently featured an enormous flat screen TV.

"Mr. Vladimir will see you in the den," the man said.

She nodded and he escorted her through the living room, and she noted the expansive kitchen that was off to the other side of the living room. She'd never seen anything so luxurious in her life. And thinking about how Igor made his money to afford all of this made her sick.

When they stopped in front of a door, she knew they were at their destination.

The guard knocked, and Igor's voice rang out loudly inviting her in.

She gave herself one more mini pep talk and walked through the door. Igor was seated at a desk with a pile of papers in front of him. Tonight he wore glasses, which made him look older. He stood up and walked over to greet her.

The guard put her gun down on Igor's desk out of her immediate reach.

"Ms. Lane. I am so glad you made it." He kissed her on the cheek, and it took every ounce of willpower she had not to cringe.

"Me, too. Although, I had quite an interesting time getting here." She eyed the man that had brought her in. She didn't know what his role was here. "Can we talk alone?"

"Of course, of course. Leave us, Dmitri. I'll be perfectly fine with Ms. Lane."

Dmitri raised an eyebrow but did as he was directed. She was now alone with Igor. Completely alone.

"Do you need your gun, Ms. Lane?" His eyes diverted to the gun in front of him. He took the gun and placed it behind him on the shelf.

She laughed. "I always need my gun." Instead of waiting for him to say anything else, she wondered if she would be able to get around him to get to her gun. Then once it was in her hands, it would only take her a second to pull her gun and shoot him in cold blood—the same way he had shot her parents. Leaving an eight-year-old girl orphaned. But she couldn't do it. She remembered the Bible verse, "Vengeance is mine…saith the Lord." She had to remind herself of that all too often.

"Please have a seat." He motioned for her to take a seat at a very large plush maroon chair across from his desk. "Tell me what is going on."

"Igor," she said, purposely using his first name. "Someone tried to follow us to the hotel. It took quite a bit of maneuvering to get away from them."

His eyes flashed with anger. "Are you sure?"

"Yes. I'm hoping, given our business arrangement that it wasn't one of your men. I'd hate to break off our business dealings before they even start. But I don't like being threatened." She kept her voice steady and didn't break eye contact.

"I can assure you, it wasn't my doing." He removed his glasses.

"Maybe you need to take a closer look at your men. Someone might have gone off the grid."

He laughed. "Nonsense. My men are loyal."

"Everyone thinks that, Igor. But we all have a price."

He slowly nodded. "Where is your FBI friend?"

"Given the circumstances, I didn't feel comfortable bringing him up here. But don't worry. I have all the information you need. And then some."

He leaned forward in his chair. "You have me intrigued, Ms. Lane."

"There's an FBI surveillance team monitoring your every move. They think you have business across the border. They're already gathering evidence of your cross-border dealings."

"Interesting."

"I want to assist in these operations in Mexico. You need me."

He cocked his head to the side. "And why would a strong woman want to get involved in that business? I'd assume you'd have quite a distaste for that enterprise."

"I'm interested in making smart business deals. That's it." She was holding her own. He seemed to be buying it. "I'd like to take a look at your setup down there. I might have some ideas to make things run more smoothly. I'd want an appropriate cut of the business, of course."

"What's in it for me?"

"A better operation. And more inside information from my friend Kip."

"Is he more than a friend?"

"That is none of your business." She tried to use her best tough girl voice.

"Ah. You are a fascinating woman, Ms. Lane."

"There's more."

"Really?"

"You need to watch out for your brother."

"My brother? What do you mean?" His eyes widened. She could tell she finally struck a nerve with him.

"My sources tell me that he is making his move against you. I wouldn't be surprised if he was the one informing the FBI of your dealings."

He slammed his fist down on his desk. "He would never work with the Feds. Ever. It's simply impossible. Unthinkable!"

"You can choose to ignore my warning if you want. I'm just providing you with the information." She leaned back in her seat.

"What else do you know?"

She didn't immediately respond. Igor walked over to her and pulled her up out of the chair. Then he slammed her roughly up against the wall, his hands closing tightly around her neck. He could kill her right now with his bare hands. He squeezed applying pressure. Fear shot through her. She needed to fight back.

Before she could make a move, he dropped his hands from her body and took a step back adjusting his jacket. She reached up and touched her throat where he'd choked her. His imprint felt burned on to her skin. He was pure evil. She had to keep it together. He had a temper, and he was trying to unravel her. Intimidate her. She was not going to cave to this man. She refused to be hurt by him anymore.

"I don't have many specifics. I'm working on it. I wanted you to know a little of what I've learned from my friend. It's no secret that the two of you are in a power struggle. What better way to take over than by framing you? Then the family business is all his."

"Why haven't I heard any of this?"

"Maybe your men don't want to give you bad news. Another reason why you need someone objective who has the resources to give you the information they don't have or won't tell you. Don't forget I'm also being paid for my work. Including my help with the Mexico operation. Are you ready to move forward?"

He paused and looked at her. Then he stepped away and took a seat back behind the desk. "You can check out my base in Mexico. Provide me with a report back. We can take it from there."

"Glad this worked out. I plan to get started right away with a trip across the border."

"And, Ms. Lane. If you hear any more about my brother, I want to hear about it. Do you understand? No delays. That takes priority over any other work you're doing for me."

"Of course."

"I wonder why you even need your FBI friend? You seem to have it very much under control."

"He has internal resources that I don't have."

"Good enough." He scribbled down something on paper and handed it to her. "This is where my operations are based in Mexico. But I'm warning you, Ms. Lane. I do not want you to come back complaining to me about the conditions down there. As you said, this is a business deal. There is no time for emotion. I usually don't work with women—so don't disappoint me."

"You won't be disappointed," she said sharply.

He nodded. "Also, I have plenty of friends in Mexico. So if you have any bright ideas about moving in on my operation or anything like that. I will simply have them kill you. Makes no difference to me."

He pressed a button on his phone and within a few seconds Dmitri walked back into the room. Then Igor reached behind him grabbing her gun from the ledge. He handed it to Dmitri who then gave it to her. She tried not to let out a breath. Feeling so much more secure armed. But she wouldn't be able to breathe normally again until she stepped out of that penthouse.

Dmitri opened the front door for her, and she stepped out in the main hallway and eagerly pushed the elevator button. She'd done it!

She rode down to the lobby and saw Kip right when she exited.

He strode over to her, his eyes wide. "You okay?"

"Yes. Let's get out of here."

Kip looked at her. "Sadie, what did he do to you?"

She looked down and although she couldn't see it, she realized her neck had to be red from Igor's nasty grip. "He choked me a little. But nothing I couldn't handle."

Kip blew out a breath. "This is getting too dangerous. I should've never allowed you to go up there alone."

"It's over now, Kip. We need to move on and focus on helping Megan."

"I've been doing some recon. I don't think our tail is

still around. But just in case. I've called in a favor. We're going to swap cars a bit down the highway."

"Someone you can trust?"

"Yes."

"Are you completely positive about that?"

"I'm sure," he said.

Once in the car, she leaned back her head and let out a deep breath. She finally felt safe. For now.

He glanced over her way. "Tell me about Igor's Mexico operation."

"I have an address in Mexico. It's outside the city of Chihuahua. Have you heard of it?"

"Yeah, that's actually where the little dog got its name from. The city is about four hours away from El Paso."

"We should cross the border tonight. There's no point in waiting."

"My friend will meet us about a mile or so from here. We'll switch cars and be good to go. What else happened at the meeting?"

Thoughts swirled through her mind. "It was a bit surreal. The penthouse was out of this world. He had a security guy at the door. But I didn't see anyone else. Granted, I only saw part of the penthouse. I'm sure he had more men stationed elsewhere."

"Where did you have the meeting?"

"In the den. His guard followed me in, but was dismissed after I told Igor I wanted to talk to him alone. I made the pitch about Mexico, and at first he seemed hesitant. But once I gave him the tidbit about Artur selling him out, that pushed him over the edge."

"That's when he got violent."

"You should've seen the look on his face. He was outraged. That's when he came at me. I think we've crossed a line into delicate territory for him. A real hot button issue. He's sensitive about his family. Something we should probably keep in mind going forward."

"Hold that thought. We're about to do the exchange."

"At the gas station?"

"Yeah. If you need anything, stock up. That's our new ride over there." He pointed at a dark SUV. "When you come back out of the store just get in the passenger seat. I'll be there waiting and will have transferred our bags."

She glanced over at the SUV. A tall blond man with a buzz cut stepped out of the car. Everything about him screamed military. He didn't even look over their way. Taking her time, Sadie stepped out of the car throwing her purse over her shoulder.

The gas station wasn't busy. She perused the aisles and picked up a couple bags of chips that she didn't need. As she stood deciding between energy bars or candy, she felt a strange prickle of awareness. The store was eerily quiet. Too quiet. Before she could act, a man's strong hand grabbed on to her from behind, covering her mouth. His other hand clutched her arm.

"Don't say a word," the deep voice said, his hot breath hit her neck. She couldn't panic.

"We're going to walk right out of here. Easy. If you do what I say, I won't hurt you." His grip on her arm made her realize he was probably lying. He was already hurting her.

This must've been the guy who had been following

them earlier. She had no idea what he wanted. Leaving with him was simply not an option. Her gun was in her purse hanging over her shoulder. No way could she get to it. She couldn't believe she'd let down her guard over some stupid candy bars.

"Walk. Slowly," he said in a voice gruff.

This could get ugly. She looked over and saw that the cashier was slumped over the checkout counter with blood trickling from his head. This guy had probably knocked him out. Surveying her surroundings, she saw there were no other people in the store. With each millisecond that passed, she knew she had to act. There was no time to waste. She said a prayer and made her move.

She stomped down on his right foot with all of her might. He yelled but only tightened his grip as he cursed at her.

After struggling to get away, she took a few steps. But he was right there. Her hip bones slammed into the checkout counter as he pushed her forward.

"I told you not to do this," he growled.

But she was far from done. When he came at her from behind and wrapped his arms around her, she kicked backward hard, landing a direct blow to his kneecap.

He howled in pain.

It was time to get out of there. She almost made it to the door when he grabbed her ankle. She hit the linoleum floor with a thud, pain shooting through her right arm that she'd used to brace the fall.

He climbed on top of her back and pulled her to her feet. This was it. She prayed for strength as she elbowed him in the solar plexus. His grip loosened. She quickly turned and punched him in the nose hearing a crunch of bone.

Then she ran.

FIVE

Kip didn't know what was taking Sadie so long. She should be done by now. He definitely didn't take her for a female who'd spend time primping in the ladies room. Something was off. He stepped out of the SUV and walked toward the front door of the gas station store. That's when he saw Sadie running toward him. A large man followed close, right behind her.

With adrenaline pumping through his veins, he ran in her direction, his gun drawn.

"Hurry," he yelled at her.

Sadie's attacker stopped when he saw Kip approaching. Not wanting to use lethal force, Kip tackled him to the ground. They both landed on the asphalt with a thump.

A wrestling match ensued, and Kip quickly had the upper hand. Kip held him down. "Who sent you?"

The man shook his head. Not responding.

"Tell me," he said.

The man let out a deep breath. "I work for Igor."

"Why did Igor send you after her?"

"He didn't. I don't trust her. And I don't trust you either." The man spit in his face.

Kip wasn't deterred. "Why does it matter to you?"

"Because if I can prove my worth to Igor by exposing traitors, I will be his next in command."

Kip couldn't help but have a tiny ounce of pity for this poor excuse for a man. He would never be Igor's number two. Kip could tell that he wasn't that bright. He was hired muscle. And wouldn't be anything more.

"If you leave right now, we won't tell Igor about this. But if you ever, and I mean ever, try to hurt Sadie again, I will track you down. Understood?"

The man groaned and nodded quickly. Kip pulled him up off the ground. "Now, go!"

He watched as the man ran off toward a small truck and drove away quickly.

That was far too close of a call. Kip jogged back to the SUV and opened the driver's side door. Sadie was sitting there trying to catch her breath.

"I thought I might need to drive," she said.

"No." He shook his head. "Are you hurt? Do you need the hospital?"

"No. I'll just be sore and bruised. This will not stop us from saving Megan."

"What happened back there?" He reached out and touched her check.

Her shoulders slumped, and she pushed the hair that had fallen out of her ponytail out of her face, and made contact with his hand. Then, she stepped slowly out of the car and walked around to get into the passenger seat.

They drove in silence for a few minutes.

"I was standing there debating between candy bars and energy bars. I was craving chocolate and wasn't paying attention because the store was so empty. By the time I sensed him behind me it was too late. He grabbed me. Told me he didn't want to hurt me, but that I had to come with him."

"Then what did you do?"

"Well, obviously, I wasn't going to just go along with that. I couldn't get to my gun, but I was able to get the drop on him and stomp down on his foot hard enough to loosen his grip. But he got to me again. There was a skirmish. I hit the ground hard. I finally was able to land a few blows. That's when I ran away. You know the rest."

"It was one of Igor's guys."

"What?" she questioned abruptly. "No, that doesn't make sense."

"It's not what you think. He said that Igor didn't tell him to do it. He just didn't like us. Didn't trust us. He thought he could get something out of you and then show Igor that you were a traitor."

"Enemies are everywhere. Even when you don't realize it."

"Yeah, I know. And this guy was just a bit too close to the truth. He won't be bothering us again. I made the consequences of future actions quite clear. And what's more, now we know who was tailing us."

"I think I recognized him from the meeting the first night at Sala. It didn't register at the time, but I think that was him. He was one of the men in Igor's security detail."

"You still up for this?"

"Are you kidding me? Of course I am. It'll take a lot more than being attacked by one useless thug for me to give up on Megan—and the other girls. Igor basically told me it was going to be a nasty scene. He didn't want me complaining to him about his business."

"He's a piece of work, Sadie. And he's right. The conditions are going to be deplorable. You need to be mentally prepared."

"Just because I'm a woman doesn't mean that I'm not tough. I will tell you now, and I don't want to have to say it again. I can handle this."

He dropped his right hand from the wheel and gently touched her knee. "I didn't mean to offend you, Sadie. You are a very tough woman. Tougher than most men. But when you start dealing with human trafficking, that's hard for anyone to stomach. No matter who you are."

"Sounds like you have experience."

"I saw some awful things while I was deployed. Things that still haunt me."

She looked over at him, and he tried to keep his focus on the dark road. "Anything you want to talk about?"

"Not particularly."

"If you keep it all bottled in, it will eventually destroy you."

"I'll be fine." He didn't even believe the words as he said them.

"I'm here if you want to talk."

"I don't even know how to begin, Sadie. I've been very lost for a long time. God wasn't listening to me. And I felt that I was abandoned when I needed Him most."

She sighed. "Kip, you're talking in riddles. It would probably be more productive if you just said what's on your mind. I'm not here to judge you. Just to listen. As a friend."

"I don't know if I'm ready to have that conversation yet."

"That's okay," she relented. "I won't push you. But know if you want to pray together, I'm here for you."

He was truly touched. No woman had ever offered to pray with him—besides his grandmother. "You're a very intriguing woman, Sadie."

"I guess I should take that as a compliment?" She laughed.

"Yes, it was meant that way. Can I ask you a personal question now?"

"Sure, why not?"

"Why are you still single? I mean, it has to be by choice. You're smart, beautiful and funny. Why choose to be alone?"

She paused for a minute. The only sound he heard was the hum of the air conditioning.

"Sometimes it's easier to only depend on yourself. People have a way of letting you down."

He nodded. "That I can relate to." He thought she was going to follow up with more questions, but she didn't. It was one of the things he liked about her. She knew when to push him and when to stop. It was a strange feeling because it seemed like he had known her for a much longer time. He had to keep reminding himself, though, that as nice as she was, he wasn't in a position to open up his heart again. And what could he offer a woman like Sadie? He was damaged goods. Severely damaged.

He wondered why she was so quiet, and then he looked over and saw her eyes were closed. She had to be exhausted. He had no plans to wake her up. She needed to rest. The remainder of this trip wasn't going to be easy. When he'd told her that he'd seen awful things while deployed, he couldn't even begin to give her the details. The slaughter he'd witnessed in the village in Iraq had been brutal. And there was nothing he could do to stop it. In fact, he'd been ordered not to intervene.

He'd considered disobeying a direct order and living with the consequences, but he also knew that one man couldn't stop the carnage. It would've taken his whole team. And after they voted, he was outnumbered. He also wasn't the highest ranked member in the group. So that was the end. He had to witness a massacre, and there was absolutely nothing he could do about it. He had to remind himself that Brad wasn't a man of faith. He was guided by principles that worked for him, but he didn't answer to the Lord. Kip couldn't help the sinking feeling in his gut that Brad just didn't want to risk his own life to save the villagers. The guilt ate at him. *God, I need You to help me.*

He sucked in a breath. Had he just prayed? He honestly couldn't remember the last time he'd said a prayer. Maybe Sadie was rubbing off on him. In a good way.

Sadie felt something nudge her arm. She went for her gun but then realized it was in her purse on the floor.

"Sadie, it's okay. It's Kip. You're safe."

His calm voice washed over her. "How long was I asleep?"

"About four hours. We're about to reach our destination."

"What time is it?"

"About two in the morning."

She groaned. "I'm listening."

"We have two options. Find a hotel in the city and get some sleep. Or we can try to check out the facility now while it's dark and get some sleep after."

"I'm worried about you. You haven't had any rest at all. I'm fine with either option."

He laughed. "Sadie, I've gone without sleep for five straight days before. I'm sure I can handle this."

She should've known that a former army ranger wouldn't slow down on a mission. "I think we check out the situation now while it's dark. Any guess on security level?"

"Actually, I'm thinking it may be pretty light. A couple of armed men are probably all that it takes. This isn't a resource intensive business. Or at least it shouldn't be if he wants this business venture to be profitable."

She shuddered at the thought of those men and what they could be doing to those poor girls. And that's exactly what most of them probably were. Girls. Not women. Megan Milton was only sixteen years old.

"You still with me, Sadie?" he asked. He reached over and gently touched her shoulder.

"Sorry. Yeah. What's the plan?"

"We'll leave the car a ways out. Then go on foot. Best case scenario is we take the guards out with nonlethal force. Then secure Megan."

"What about the others? We can't just leave them there."

"I know. We'll try our best to get them all out. But depending on the numbers we might not have immediate transport capability for them all. Once we figure out exactly what we're dealing with, I can patch in the Mexican police forces who work with the FBI. I've got full FBI backing."

"I take it that all Mexican police aren't friendly to American interests."

"You got that right."

They drove in silence while Sadie mentally took stock of the situation. Kip's eyes were intent on the road. They were both focused on what they needed to accomplish.

Kip stopped the car. "From here we go on foot." He pulled something out of his pocket.

"You have a GPS?"

"Yeah, a nifty navigator. Plus an old-school compass because I roll like that." He smiled before he opened the door to the SUV. He was trying to lighten the mood, but nothing could make her feel any better right now. Darkness enveloped her as she stepped out of the car.

Kip came fully prepared with high-tech night vision goggles that also operated as binoculars. She had her regular night vision goggles, and she was again thankful for them. Because if they hadn't had their equipment, it would probably be impossible to see anything. This wasn't a big city with street lights, but a rural area on the outskirts of town. The summer heat was brutal even at night. She felt a trickle of sweat roll down her back as they started walking through the darkness.

He took her hand and squeezed. "We've got this. Stay close. And don't make any moves without me. Got it?"

"Yes, sir," she snapped. She didn't mean it to come out so curt, but she was getting a little tired of taking orders from Kip. She was used to being her own woman, her own boss. It was clear to her that he only knew how to operate if he was the one running the show. But she couldn't lose sight of the bigger picture. Right now she needed to concentrate on rescuing Megan.

"Hey, I'm sorry." He grabbed her arm gently. "I know I can be bossy. Especially on a mission. Even though

I'm out of the army, I haven't lost my military training and the take-charge mentality."

"I understand. Let's stay on task."

He pushed a stray hair out of her face, and she felt the warmth of his touch. He was a good man, as much as he might irritate her sometimes, she couldn't deny that. And she had her own control issues. She couldn't help but laugh thinking about it. Her issues were probably worse than his.

"What's so funny?"

"Oh, nothing. Just thinking that you and I are actually very similar."

"You think so?"

"Yes," she said. She tripped over something. "Ouch." He grabbed on to her arm, steadying her.

"You all right?"

"Yeah. I don't know what that was. Probably some stray debris or a root."

"I think we're getting close." He looked through his special night vision binoculars. "Yeah. I see some type of warehouse up ahead. We'll need to go silent. Only talk if absolutely necessary. We'll use simple hand signals as much as possible." He stopped and turned toward her. "If that sounds good to you? Let me know if you have other ideas."

He was making an effort to include her. "Hand signals it is," she said softly.

She didn't know how it was possible, but it seemed to only get darker which each step. A chill went down her neck even with the blistering heat. This was it.

He made a sweeping motion toward himself with his hand, signaling her to stick close. He didn't have to worry about that. She didn't have any intention of running off on her own right now. She might prefer to work independently, but she surely wasn't stupid.

She gasped at what she saw in front of her. This couldn't be right. Her heartbeat raced. Kip squeezed her shoulder. Then he signaled no. He must have seen it, too. Because this wasn't just a warehouse with two armed guards. No, there were multiple men. All armed with automatic weapons.

Kip tugged on her arm. It was clear he wanted to retreat. But she shook her head no. She pulled him close and whispered in his ear. "We need to understand what we're up against. Let me go get a better look. I'll be right back." She took a step.

"No." He pulled her back, and spoke in her ear. "Absolutely not. I'm not letting you out of my sight. This just got a lot more dangerous. Those men all have submachine guns, all automatic weapons. There's a lot more taking place here than what we anticipated." He spoke so low she could barely hear him, but she felt his warm breath tickling her ear.

"Let's just get a little closer. Please." She tugged on his arm.

It must have been the please that did it, because he nodded. They walked very slowly and crouched down low to the ground. Quickly she pulled out her night vision camera that had cost her more than two months' mortgage payment, and snapped a few pictures with the nighttime setting. There was no way that many armed men with high power weaponry would be needed to guard a group of girls. Something else was going on here. What had they walked into? And more importantly, why did Igor send her here? Was it all an elaborate trap?

Kip nudged her shoulder, and she knew it was time to fall back. They had some serious regrouping to do.

Something caught her attention out of the corner of her eye. But it was too late. The guard was right there. And he had his submachine gun pointed in their direction. He didn't have on night vision goggles so it's likely they were only shadows to him.

"Que hay?" the guard asked.

He was asking who was there. He started walking in their direction. Then she felt a large hand on her arm. She didn't scream. Instead she punched him hard. She connected with his jaw. The man grunted in pain.

Then Kip lunged toward the man slamming him to the ground. Thankfully the gun didn't go off. With one punch, Kip knocked him out.

She squatted down to the ground. "Is he conscious?" she asked.

Kip stood up. "No. Between the impact and the punch, he's out. But we need to get out of here."

They moved quickly on foot back to the SUV, jogging in silence. Once inside, she leaned her head back against the seat. "What just happened out there?"

"Nothing good."

"Why would Igor have given me this address?" She was so confused.

"Maybe he's testing you."

"How so?"

"He wants to know if you're really legit or if this is all a ruse. Igor's no dummy. We provided him a very neatly tied up story. He's probably skeptical."

"On the other hand, if he believes that we are who we say we are, then he should want to work with us. It still doesn't make sense. We could've gotten killed."

"I suppose it's possible that he told them we might be coming. It's good they didn't actually see us. That guard didn't have on night vision goggles. No way would he be able to identify us. He probably couldn't even tell that we were male and female. Just two bodies, since it was so dark."

"You're forgetting about Megan. Where is she? Where are the others?" She could hear the strain in her own voice.

He sighed. "Sadie, I don't know. The extra security may have nothing to do with the trafficking of the girls. I just don't know."

"Even if that's the case, it's not going to help us find Megan." Her heart sunk, as the realization of her own words crept in. Lord, what were they going to do? *Please,* she prayed. *Those girls need us.* "We have to think," she said. More to herself than to him.

He had grown very quiet. She looked at him, and he simply stayed focused on the road as they drove back toward the city.

"Hey," she said with a start, as an idea popped into her head. "What if those weren't Igor's men?"

"How do you figure that?" He tapped his fingers on the steering wheel.

"What if they found out what he was doing and took over? Or shut him down?"

"Why would they do that?"

"Maybe a turf war. The Mexican drug lords are notorious for protecting their turf—at any cost."

"How do you know so much about that?"

"I had a cop friend who worked on the border. I heard a lot of stories from him."

"A boyfriend?"

Intrigued by his continued interest in her romantic history, she answered truthfully. “No, just a friend.”

“Your theory is that Igor’s operation here has been compromised by the local forces?”

“It’s just one idea. I can’t believe Igor would’ve sent me into that. If he wanted to kill me, he could’ve easily done that in his penthouse. I know he probably distrusts us, but I can’t help but feeling that he actually likes me. It makes no sense that he would’ve wanted me ambushed. Especially after I gave him the rundown on Artur. He definitely wanted to hear more about that. Almost desperately so. He said it took precedence over anything else I was working on.”

“We need to make a decision. Do we report this to Igor, assuming your theory is correct? Or do we wait?”

“If we wait, we run the risk of him finding out that we knew something was awry and didn’t report it.” She took a moment and ran through the scenarios in her head. “I think we call him.”

“It’s risky, Sadie” he said softly.

“The alternative’s worse. I need to get to Megan. He’s our best chance to figure out where she could be.”

“When do you want to make the call?”

“Now.”

“Don’t you think he’ll find it a little odd that you ran down here right after your meeting?”

“No. I told him I was taking a trip right away. He probably didn’t realize I meant tonight, but I think it’s fine. I’d rather get out ahead of this thing.”

“You’re going to wake him up.”

“Probably. But, Kip, I don’t care. He’ll answer if he wants.”

“You ready to do it?”

"Yes. I'll put him on Speaker." She pulled out her cell. She felt like she was doing the right thing.

It rang three times, and then a raspy voice answered. "This better be good."

"Igor, it's Sadie."

"What's going on?" He demanded.

"I'm down here in Mexico. And I paid a visit to your facility." She paused hoping that he was following her. "Imagine my surprise when I saw a whole cadre of armed men with automatic weapons parading around."

"What? My warehouse only has a few guards in rotation twenty-four hours a day. They certainly don't carry automatic weapons. You're wrong."

"I don't like being sent into a trap, Igor," she said as sternly as possible.

"I did not send you into a trap," he said, his voice raised. "Tell me again what you saw. Are you sure you were at the correct location?"

"I went to the exact coordinates you provided me."

"How many men?"

"Probably fifteen or so. All armed with automatic weapons. Clearly that type of force isn't needed to guard any type of operation that we discussed."

"No. Of course not. Ms. Lane, ever since you came into my life, very strange things have been happening. Doesn't that seem odd to you?"

She had to keep her cool and play it smart. "Igor, I don't think I'm the problem. I think you have to get a better grip on your business investments. There is something going on down here in Mexico. If I had to guess, I'd say the men I saw are part of the local Mexican drug cartels. Maybe they don't want you moving in on their territory. I'd need more intel than what I have right now in order to provide sound advice. Regardless, I don't know the status of your merchandise." It killed her inside to refer to those poor girls that way, but she had to be convincing.

"Ms. Lane. I need you to figure out what's going on down there. Is your friend with you?"

"Yes."

"Can the two of you handle this yourselves? I would send additional resources, but it looks like I'll be short-staffed after I finish showing my current employees what happens when they don't follow orders. I won't have my people working for the local drug lords. They must be loyal to me. And now they will pay. If you are successful, you will be more than adequately rewarded. I need answers, Ms. Lane. And I need them fast."

"Yes. We're on it."

"I'll send you the contact information for one of my friends in the Mexican police force. His name is Jorge Valez. He can be trusted. Beyond him, I can't say. You're on your own. I'd tell you to be careful. But I won't second-guess your abilities."

She couldn't believe this was happening. How was she actually working with this man? The man who had killed her family. She clenched her fists feeling her short nails push into her flesh as her hands shook. Then Megan's face popped in her head—the picture of the girl who'd already had a rough life at sixteen. Now being held hostage by these monsters.

"Ms. Lane?"

"Yes, I'm here."

"You did the right thing by contacting me. Keep up the good work. Stay in touch. And remember to call me right away if you hear anything else about my brother. I want you to send me any evidence you find immediately."

"Will do." She pressed the button to disconnect and let out a huge sigh of relief. She was still shaking.

Kip reached over and grabbed her hand, instantly steadying her. "You handled him very well. Sounded to me like he was truly surprised. That would be some pretty amazing dramatics if he was acting."

"What have we gotten in the middle of?"

"A turf war and who knows what else." He let go of her hand and she realized how much she enjoyed his touch. Even though she didn't want to.

After driving back into the city, they pulled up into a hotel parking lot.

"This hotel looks good," he said. "If they have the option we'll get two adjoining rooms. That okay with you?"

"Yeah." She looked up at the large hotel. It was definitely not the five-star Rhubarb Hotel, but it was nice and in the middle of the city. She could use a few hours of sleep, and she knew that Kip definitely could. He might act tough and macho, but he wasn't invincible. They both needed to be on the top of their game to hunt down Megan.

By the time they'd gotten to their rooms, exhaustion had taken over. The adrenaline rush was long gone.

"I'll be right next door if you need anything," Kip said.

"I'll be fine." But she had to admit she felt better knowing he was right next door. "How long are we sleeping?"

"How much sleep do you need?"

"No. You tell me. I'll make it work."

"Set an alarm for nine a.m."

"Okay." They had a full day of work ahead of them.

He walked over and gave her a big hug. "You did great work today. I'm happy to have you as my partner."

That was the biggest compliment he could've paid her. She wanted him to see her as an equal, a true partner. Although, the feeling deep in her gut had her wanting even more from him. She quickly pushed that aside. There was no way they would work out as a couple.

"I'll close the adjoining door, but leave it unlocked."

She nodded. He turned and walked away, and she felt a sense of loneliness. She desperately needed sleep. Hopefully, she'd have a clearer head after that. Especially about Kip. She couldn't engage in these foolish daydreams.

Rummaging through her bag, she found some pajamas and put them on. She pulled back the fluffy comforter and fell into the soft bed. While the bed was super comfortable, her mind was racing. How could she enjoy all of these comforts when Megan was out there in danger? She felt sick just thinking about it. Logically, she knew she needed to get rest so she would be on top of her game, but she couldn't fall asleep.

And then there was Kip. She hadn't quite figured him out. He definitely had issues—both with God and his time in the military and who knows what else. She couldn't blame him for being haunted by the horrors of war. She hoped that even if it was only in a small way, that their discussions about faith could help him. If it wasn't for her faith, she would've given up a long time ago. Her adoptive parents loved her so much. And what they gave to her in terms of leading by example was priceless. Her relationship with God was what it was today because of them.

Igor's face invaded her thoughts. This time it wasn't Igor from the Rhubarb Hotel, but the young Igor that had shot her parents in cold blood.

Could she truly trust Kip? He was an FBI agent, which of course made him suspect from the start, but she believed he had integrity instilled in him through his time in the service. Hopefully, the FBI hadn't corrupted him. What would he do when he found out who she really was? And that she had a history with Igor? She couldn't let that happen. That was another reason why she couldn't get any silly ideas in her head about them starting a relationship. She'd not given him the whole story—far from it. If he had found out the truth, there was no way he would've teamed up with her. But so far, she was keeping it together. For the sake of Megan and the others girls, she had to. As much as she wanted personal revenge on Igor, that could wait. It had to wait. Because innocent lives were at stake.

SIX

Kip was in the all too familiar nightmare. And he knew there was no way out. Not yet. The hot desert sand whirled around him with the sun beating down against his roughened skin. The sounds of the Blackhawk helicopter pounded in his ears as he looked up and saw it descending into the desert. Fallujah was about the worst place on earth. And of course he was right in the middle of it.

They were on a mission going building to building searching for the enemy. Unfortunately for him, the enemy was living among the innocent civilian population. One wrong shot and he could kill an innocent person. Or worse, a child. Rapid shots rang out through the hot air. Someone yelled to take cover. An explosion rocked the earth. His ears rang. So loud. He tasted blood. "No," he screamed. He tried to run, but his legs were pinned under rubble. He screamed again. Someone was calling his name. A woman was calling his name. Was she hurt?

"Kip," the voice said. "Wake up. Kip."

He couldn't break out of it. Not yet. He had to find the woman.

"Kip." The female's voice was growing louder. As if she was right there, speaking into his ear. Then her hands. They were on his shoulders.

He was free. His eyes opened, and then he saw her. Sadie. He'd been having a nightmare…again.

"Are you okay?" she asked.

He paused. "Yeah," he said softly.

"You were screaming. I thought at first someone had gotten in here and attacked you."

He looked over and noticed her gun sitting on his bed beside her.

"I'm sorry. It was just a nightmare."

"Anything you want to talk about right now?"

He was really embarrassed. This was another reason he didn't want to have a wife. Couldn't have a wife. She'd have to be subjected to his recurring nightmares. He shook his head and looked over at the clock. They'd only been asleep for about three hours. "No. Let's just try to go back to sleep."

She frowned. He could tell she wanted to say something but was holding back. She relented and stood up from his bed. "See you in a few hours," she said quietly. She shut the adjoining door behind her.

He was a wreck. Maybe now that she'd seen what a mess he was, she'd put out of her mind any ideas of getting closer to him. He couldn't miss that look in her eyes when he'd told her good night a few hours ago. It was a look he hadn't seen in a very long time. She had some level of interest in him. After tonight that was surely squelched. And that was probably for the best.

He knew himself well enough to know that there was most likely no more sleep after that nightmare. But he made himself stay in bed and close his eyes. Maybe he could will himself to sleep. As he lay there in the dark room, his thoughts went back to Iraq. To Brad. And of course, to his ex-fiancée. Brad had been at home rehabbing during Kip's final deployment, and that's when he had made his advances on Lacy. Lacy had all too willingly accepted them. She'd torn out his heart in the process. Robbed him of everything he valued. The person he loved, the job he was devoted to, and the ranger teammates he thought of as family, not to mention his relationship with God. Now look at him. Pathetic.

A combination of pain and emptiness filled him. He closed his eyes. Would God hear him if he prayed? His faith had once been so strong. Strong enough to get him through too many nights in the desert. Strong enough to push through the grief when his brothers-in-arms died in combat. Strong enough to go into battle, knowing that day could be his last. He'd let Brad take that away from him. With all of Brad's talk of team unity. He'd been the leader, but now Kip saw the truth. It was all a ruse.

Lord...I don't know how I got so lost. But I'm hoping You will show me the way back...

Hours later, Kip opened one eye as light flooded in through the window. He was shocked that he had been able to go back to sleep. The last thing he remembered was starting to pray. He felt more rested than he had in months. Looking over at the clock, he saw that it was eight thirty. He wondered if Sadie was up yet. His stomach rumbled, reminding him of how hungry he was. What he wouldn't give for a big cup of coffee. Was it his imagination or did he smell food? And coffee?

After getting dressed, he pressed his ear to Sadie's door. He heard what sounded like the TV. He knocked lightly. She answered the door with a smile. Aha! He knew he smelled something.

On her small table, she had plates of food and a huge pot of coffee.

"I heard you knocking around in there. I was about to come get you. Breakfast just arrived." She smiled.

"You have no idea how much I appreciate this."

"Help yourself. I might have gone a little overboard, but I was hungry."

"No. I feel like I could eat it all." He laughed.

They sat down at the little table, and he took a huge gulp of coffee—enjoying the warmth of it as it hit his tongue.

"So," she said, as she speared eggs onto her fork. "Why don't we talk about last night?"

"Let's not."

"Kip, if something is bothering you so much that you have such painful deep nightmares, don't you think it's better to let it out? And don't try to brush off last night as just a one-time thing."

He rubbed his chin, and his head started to ache. But when he looked into her eyes, a little peace settled over him.

She reached over and grabbed his hand. "Kip, you said that you were glad I was your partner. You can trust me with this. If it makes you feel any better, we all have secrets. They just impact us in different ways. I won't judge you."

"I need a little more time to wrap my head around my own issues," he said honestly. "But I appreciate the offer. It's nice to have someone who listens. Really listens."

"The offer stands. I'm ready to listen whenever you're ready to talk."

"Thanks." He also needed time to figure out his growing feelings for this woman. Did she ever say or do the wrong thing?

"Ideas on our plan of action today?"

He was about to answer when he heard something. All of his senses went into high alert. He lifted up his finger to his lips. There, there it was again. Someone was trying to get into Sadie's hotel room door.

She frowned and pulled her gun from her bag on the floor beside her.

His weapon was in his room. This was no good. What a rookie mistake. Would she give him her gun?

He mouthed to her asking for her gun. She hesitated, but then handed it to him. He motioned toward his room for her to take cover. He whispered the location of his gun to her—he'd placed it under the mattress. She quickly exited through the adjoining door. Quietly he moved toward the main door of her room and then crouched down behind the small couch. Waiting for the intruder to make his move. A clicking noise was followed by the door slowly opening. Two men dressed all in black with guns walked in. This was no good.

At least Sadie was out of harm's way for the moment. He had the element of surprise on his side, and he planned to take advantage.

The two guys walked toward the couch, but they never saw him coming. Their guns were in their hands but down by their sides. So he used that to his benefit, put his gun in his waistband and relied on the one thing that was tried and true. Brute force.

He lunged out at the first man taking him out at the

legs and knocking him into the other. Their weapons hit the floor. But one of the men was quick to get to his feet and ready to fight.

Kip punched him hard, connecting with his jaw sending the man tumbling back to the ground. The other man jumped on Kip's back and tightly squeezed his arms around his neck. But Kip was strong enough to step back toward the wall and slam the man into it to loosen his grip. He hit the ground with a thud.

Kip drew his weapon. "Don't move, either of you."

Sadie stepped into the room where Kip was standing with his gun drawn, holding the two men captive.

She closed the door, and all eyes went to her. The taller man standing closer to her dove right at her. Knocking her down hard, she lost her grip on Kip's gun. It slid across the floor out of her reach. The assailant must not have been expecting the momentum from the impact because he fell to the ground, too. He started to get up. But not wasting a second, she slammed her forearm into his throat knocking him back down.

That gave her the moment she needed to grab the gun. "Stop, or I'll shoot," she yelled. She pointed the gun at the man.

"Keep the gun on him," Kip told her. He ripped a sheet off the bed and tied the first man up against a chair. As he approached the second man, the man tried to make a move, but Kip was far too quick, leveling a punch knocking him out cold. Kip grimaced as he shook out his hand from the punch.

She was relieved she didn't have to shoot the guy.

Kip looked over at her. "We've got to move before they wake up. I'll tie this one up and put on the do-not-disturb sign. Hopefully that will keep them occupied for a while."

"Who do you think sent them?"

"I don't know. But we're not going to wait around for any of their friends to show up. Check to see if they have any ID. If they do, bring it with us. Gather up all your things."

She moved into high gear. She gave the first guy a little kick with her foot before she started checking his pockets. She searched his jacket and his pants. Nothing. Same for the second guy. She pulled out her camera and took pictures of their faces. Never knew when that could come in handy.

"Good thinking," he said, as he brushed by her.

"No ID."

Kip tied them up with some rope he'd brought in his backpack full of supplies. They checked the room one more time for their belongings.

"Let's get out of here," he said.

He put his arm gently on her lower back and guided her out the door.

"Keep your eyes open."

"They always are." She surveyed the surroundings, but there was nothing out of the ordinary. "How could we already have made enemies?"

"Maybe someone spotted us last night. Or at least the car. Then they traced the car here. That's my best guess. They probably wanted to know what we were up to. They probably tagged us for DEA or some other U.S. government agency."

"That would make sense if they were in the drug-running business. Are we going to need to get a new ride?"

"Eventually."

She was grateful they'd both gotten sleep last night, for she feared a long day and night ahead of them. "Igor gave me the name of someone in the local police. Maybe we should start there. Get the lay of the land. I can't help but feel like we've walked into something much bigger than we thought."

"And I don't trust Igor one bit. At this point, I don't trust anyone," he said.

"What about me?"

He laughed. "Well, I'm stuck with you at the moment."

She looked out the window as they drove through the city. "I'm not big on trusting others either. I learned a long time ago that I need to be able to trust myself. Rely on myself. I knew I'd never be as strong as those I'm up against. And I'm already small to begin with. But I realized training would help level the playing field. Not only in weapons, but in self-defense and hand-to-hand combat."

"It shows."

She laughed. "Yeah, but if you wanted to take me down, it would take you all of five seconds. If that. But I'd give the best I've got. And in general, I feel like I can protect myself around most people. You're obviously in a different category. Thankfully, most of the men I deal with are not army rangers."

"You're a great shot."

"Thanks. I work on it a lot."

"Yes, your college buddy taught you, right?"

"Yeah. A very good friend."

"What happened to him?"

"He's still around."

"Are you two serious?" he asked, looking over at her for a moment.

"No, we aren't romantically involved. Strictly platonic."

"Why?"

"For starters, he's about thirty years too old for me."

Kip laughed. "I thought you meant someone you went to school with."

"No. I met him in college. He was an instructor in my first self-defense class. A former marine and cop. He took me under his wing."

"That's great."

She didn't mention that her friend Ron also had major issues with the FBI. She longed to believe that Kip was different. But her instinctual doubt remained.

The man she saw today, and had worked with for the past twenty four hours, seemed like a different type of man. Yes, he was unbelievably strong and she knew he could use lethal force if necessary. But he was also incredibly kind to her. It warmed her heart thinking about how special he was becoming to her. Could there ever be something between them? Maybe he wouldn't want to stay in the FBI forever? Maybe it could work if he left, but could she continue to keep her secrets from him? She just couldn't see how things would work out. Like all the other times she was troubled, she'd just have to turn her questions over to God and pray on it.

"You going to make that call?" Kip asked.

"Yeah, sorry. I started daydreaming."

"About me?" he joked.

She laughed, but she felt her cheeks flush. Was he joking? She decided it was safer not to answer and looked at her cell locating the text message from Igor with Jorge's phone number.

After one ring, *"Hola,"* a male voice answered.

"Is this Jorge?"

"Who is this?"

"My name is Sadie. We have a mutual friend, Igor."

"Ah. Yes." He paused. "What can I do for you?"

"Can we meet?"

"*Sí.* Where are you?"

"Outside Chihuahua."

"Yes, I can come there. Meet me on the dirt roads off of Juevez and Alta. Are you coming alone?"

"I'm bringing my partner with me. Igor knows that we work as a team."

"I will be there in a few minutes."

She hung up and turned her attention to Kip. "Do we think this is safe?"

"Nothing is safe around here. Especially on the outskirts of town. The drug lords are in control. We need to keep a low profile. We've already stirred the pot too much as evidenced by our visitors at the hotel. Maybe Jorge can help us get a new ride."

"We need a lead on Megan. And I intend to get one."

"Be careful, Sadie. We can't blow this."

"We've wasted time we don't have."

Her phone rang, and her breath caught. "It's Ms. Milton," she said. "Hello."

"Sadie?"

"Yes, it's me. Have you heard anything else?"

"Yes. Yes. Megan called again. She's in some place in Mexico. It sounded like the dog."

"Chihuahua?"

"Yes. She heard guards talking about it."

"How does she have a phone?"

"She couldn't explain, but she said the phone was about to lose battery power and she had to talk quickly. I'm so worried. She's freaking out. What can you expect? She's sixteen. What are they going to do to my baby?" Ms. Milton sobbed openly now.

"Ms. Milton, listen to me. I'm in Mexico right now. I will do everything I can to find her. Did she describe any of her surroundings?"

"She said she was in a small old beaten-down warehouse. But that's all she knew. Please, please find her. I'm begging you. I don't know how much time she has. She thought they'd be moving them somewhere else tonight."

"I will let you know as soon as I find out anything else. And if she calls you again, call me no matter what time it is. You hear me?"

"Yes. Yes. Again, I can't thank you enough. Please bring my baby home."

Sadie hung up and tears stung her eyes. She couldn't even begin to imagine what Ms. Milton was really going through. She only understood a piece of her pain. "Kip, we've got to find Megan. How is she getting a phone to make those calls?"

"I don't know, but she might not only be saving her life but the lives of the other girls, too."

"Only if we can get to them in time."

"We will."

"Look, Kip." She pointed. "This is the dirt road turnoff."

He slowed down and sure enough another car was parked farther down the road.

"That has to be Jorge," she said. All of a sudden she

felt cold, even though it was incredibly warm. This meeting was important. Maybe they could start finding answers.

"Do you want to take the lead?" Kip asked.

His question surprised her. "Let me start. But if you feel like we're losing him, please step in."

She tried to take a few deep breaths before stepping out of the SUV. She walked beside Kip over to the man she assumed was Jorge. He was medium height and probably in his forties. His jet black hair was cut short, and he wore a short sleeved button down. Not exactly a police uniform, but it looked a bit formal for the middle of rural Mexico.

"Jorge?" she asked.

"*Sí, señorita.* You are Ms. Sadie?"

"Yes. And this is Kip."

They exchanged brief handshakes. His dark eyes narrowed, though, in apparent suspicion. "What can I do to help you?"

"What we need most is information. And Igor said you'd be the one to contact."

He laughed. "I do what I can. Igor is a tough man." He wagged his finger at her. "You do not want to cross him."

Didn't she already know that? "We're actually trying to figure out what is happening to one of his businesses down here."

"Which business?"

"I think you know which one."

He looked away averting his eyes.

"The girls," Kip said, his voice deep.

Jorge's eyes flipped back to Kip. "You don't want any part of that my friend."

"I need to know what's going on," Sadie said.

"I don't have good news for Igor, and you work with him. Yes?"

"I do," she said quickly. "But we saw some things last night that made us think that particular business has gotten wrapped up in local politics, for lack of a better word."

Jorge nodded. "Those who run things around here. They do not like that particular business."

She wanted to cut right to it. "Drug lords have some moral qualms?"

"*Sí,* they do, *señorita.* And they definitely don't want a Russian man coming down here and bringing that sort of business with him. They also believe that Mr. Vladimir will hurt their businesses. So they are trying to put a stop to his movements altogether."

"What will happen to those girls?"

"*Señorita,* I'm not sure what the plan of the locals is. All I know is they want the Russians out of here. Completely."

"I have to know about their location."

Something flashed through his eyes. A knowing sign of something that oddly put her at ease. "You will find the girls at an abandoned farmhouse. It sits behind a large warehouse. The warehouse has merchandise for the locals. It is a few miles from here." He pointed south. "But word is that they won't be there long."

"Igor said I could trust you."

"You can."

"Then why haven't you told Igor this yourself?"

He looked down as the seconds ticked by. Then he gazed back up at her. "I do what I have to do. Igor, he will come for my family or send his men. I must protect them first. But what he is doing with those girls is not right. We're a religious people down here in this city. It's wrong. And we all know it."

"And drug running isn't?"

He shrugged. "I'm going to pretend like we never had the rest of this conversation. I hope that you will report any findings to Igor based on what you see. I have a family to protect."

"I understand that, Jorge." She took his hand again and shook it.

"Jorge," Kip said. "Any way we could trade cars with you?"

Jorge looked over at the SUV then back at his older sedan. "You joke with me?"

"No. But I have to warn you. There may be some people looking for this car. We're not sure who they are or what they want. So I don't want to put you in danger."

"No, no. Don't worry about that. I'll gladly take your car. You're getting the bad part of the deal here."

They unloaded their supplies from the SUV and placed them into the sedan.

"At least it has air conditioning," Kip said.

"I wonder what Igor has on Jorge?" she asked. "He's afraid of Igor coming after his family. You could see the look of fear in his eyes. It broke my heart."

"I think men like Igor make it their business to rule by instilling fear into people."

"I find it interesting that these drug lords have some sort of moral qualm with human trafficking."

"A lot of the drug business is purely financial. I'm sure it's not all out of the goodness of their hearts, though. The bottom line is that they don't want any of

Igor's businesses taking off down here because it will impact their operations."

"We have to make our move tonight."

Sadie and Kip spent the afternoon planning their rescue operation. Kip checked in with the El Paso field office and gave them a full debrief on the situation. They had the green light to proceed. The FBI was on standby in case they were needed for an extraction.

The biggest decision was whether they go in hostile or friendly with the locals. In the end, they'd decided they couldn't trust anyone except each other.

Sadie looked at Kip. "We have no idea how many girls and women are in there. How are we going to get them out?"

"I know Megan is your top priority, but we'll do everything in our power to help them all. Regardless of how many of them there are. Until we understand what we're up against, it's hard to have a set plan."

"I guess you're right."

"You ready for this?" Kip asked.

Her heart was racing, but she was ready. "Yes."

"Remember, we go in quiet. If we can get in and out undetected, all the better. If not, anything we can do to help make it look like it was a local operation we should do."

Not wanting to take any risk, they left Jorge's car about a mile away. Kip insisted that he could carry Megan if he needed to. And she believed him.

Now crouched down behind an adjacent building, it was time. A light warm wind blew against her face. She prayed for their safety and the safety of all of the girls.

He grabbed her hand and nodded. Through her

night vision goggles she could see his calm exterior. He was in ranger mode, and she had no doubt that he was going to help them succeed on this mission. The only doubts she had were about her own abilities. This was not the time to have a panic attack. She needed to follow through and execute. Lives were at stake, and she wouldn't get a second chance. Ms. Milton's words rang loudly in her ears. *Please bring my baby home.* Sadie would do anything she could to reunite Megan with her family.

There was a high window on the back side of the farmhouse. Kip boosted her up onto his shoulders, and she braced herself for the worst. She peered into the window and gasped. A total sense of desperation filled her up. The room was empty. Completely empty. They were too late.

She patted Kip's shoulder signaling that she wanted down.

"There's no one there," she whispered in his ear.

He looked around surveying the area. Then he pointed to another building. It wasn't a farmhouse but a warehouse. One of many. Would they have to check every building in this area?

She heard voices. Female voices. She turned around and couldn't believe it. She saw a group of about twenty girls across the way walking out of one of the warehouses. They were being escorted by two men.

"C'mon. Let's follow them," Kip whispered.

Where were they taking them? Two large vans were parked about a half a mile up. That had to be it. They couldn't let those girls get in those vans.

"Vans," she said.

He nodded, and they picked up their pace to a jog.

They needed to get ahead of the group, but doing it without being detected was going to be difficult.

They decided to run around the back of one of the buildings. She was thankful she'd been keeping up her workout routine. "What do we do?"

"There's two men with the girls and another two at the vans—presumably the drivers. We split up. You take the guys at the vans, and I'll take the others. Don't shoot to kill, but do what you have to do to protect those girls. Wait as long as you can for me to act first."

She was prepared to do what she must in order to save innocent lives. She ran in front of Kip and made her way over to the vans. They had the element of surprise working in their favor. Once shots started to get fired, anything could happen.

With each step the girls took toward the van, her pulse quickened. From what she could see, none of them appeared to be injured. She thanked God for that. What in the world were they planning to do with them? Igor's hired locals were obviously not following orders.

Sadie could see Kip coming up right behind the man in the back of the group. She watched closely as Kip squeezed his arms around the man's neck in a sleeper hold using non-lethal force that crumpled him to the ground. One down.

Unfortunately, one of the girls noticed Kip and started screaming. Sadie had no choice but to act. With one decisive shot, she hit the first driver in the thigh. He cried out as he hit the ground. Quickly turning she fired a shot at the second driver—hitting him in the shoulder. Both drivers were down and incapacitated… for the moment.

Just as she was trying to catch her breath, strong

hands clamped down on her grabbing her waist and picking her up off the ground. Where had this guy come from?

His grip was powerful, but she was a fighter. She hadn't come all this way to be taken now by one of these men. Praying for strength, she elbowed him once in the stomach. He grunted but didn't loosen his hold on her.

Reaching up behind her, she clasped her hands tightly around his thick neck. He might have been stocky, but thankfully he was short. She leaned forward and, using every ounce of energy she could muster, she flipped him over her body. Once he hit the ground, she pushed her foot into his neck making sure he couldn't move. She didn't want to really hurt this man, so once he seemed to start choking, she released some of the pressure. Then picking up her gun, she hit him on the side of the head with it. *That should keep him out of a while*, she thought.

She looked over and saw Kip surrounded by the group of girls. She ran over to them. An armed man was lying on the ground and not moving thanks to another sleeper hold from Kip. They didn't have a lot of time.

Kip looked at the group of girls. "We're here to help you."

Some of them didn't believe him because they turned and were ready to bolt.

"Wait, please," she chimed in. "We are here to get you out. But we have to go now." She surveyed the group in the darkness and realized the girls didn't have the advantage of the night vision goggles.

One girl stepped forward. She looked a bit older and taller than the rest of them. "I'm in charge here," she said.

Sadie was struck by the idea that they had a leader. She couldn't imagine what all they'd gone through.

"Are you all American?"

"Yes," the tall girl said.

"Which one of you is Megan?"

No one answered. The tall girl spoke. "Who are you?" she asked.

"I'm a private investigator. I was hired by Megan's mom. But we want to help all of you. Can you drive?" she asked.

"Duh, I'm seventeen. Of course I can drive."

"Good, you're taking that first van." She didn't even mind the sassy teenage response. At this point, she was grateful for it. "You're going to take a group of girls with you and follow us toward the border. We'll lead you to an FBI liaison who will escort you back into the U.S. Can someone else drive the second van?"

Another girl stepped forward.

"Do not stop for anyone," Sadie directed. "And stay with us."

She heard Kip already talking to his FBI contact on the phone and updating his team on the situation.

"I need to know who Megan is. Her mom is worried sick."

Finally, a short brunette toward the back stepped forward. "I'm Megan."

"You're coming with us. Everyone, we have to get out of here now. It's not safe. These guards will not stay down forever, and who knows if there are reinforcements."

They piled all the girls into the two vans. To have been through so much, the girls seemed remarkably calm and lucid.

"Thank you so much for getting us out of this. We didn't know what was next," the tall girl said.

"The FBI is on its way to the border. They'll signal you with their lights. Four quick flashes. Only stop if you see that signal."

"You don't have to worry about us stopping for any other reason."

"You're doing a great job." Sadie patted the girl on the shoulder as she stepped into the driver's seat of the van.

"Where are we going?" Megan asked Sadie.

"Home, Megan. We're taking you home."

SEVEN

Megan sat quietly in the backseat of the sedan. Sadie couldn't really blame her. She didn't want to push, but she needed to know what had happened. They'd met up with the FBI escort, and he was taking the other girls on a different route just to be on the safe side.

Sadie decided to try to break the ice. "How did you make those phone calls to your mom?"

Megan sighed. "The idiot guy who was watching us left his phone lying around. We were all scared of him at first, but then we realized he wasn't that bright."

"Since we've got a little time as we drive back. Can you tell me what happened? Lauren told me that the two of you were at Sala for a special dinner. She said she left for a few minutes and when she returned she couldn't find you."

"It was so scary at first," Megan said softly. "One minute I was sitting at our table listening to the band, and the next thing I know some guy had his hands on me. He had a gun to my side and told me I had to go with him or he would shoot. Then once we were outside, I turned around, and he put something on my mouth. I woke up later. I was in the back of a big truck with the other girls. We'd all been kidnapped. Many of the girls were taken from a group foster home outside El Paso. I thought Lauren might have been captured, too, but once I looked at everyone I realized that she wasn't there."

"I'm so sorry."

"We weren't stupid. We knew what could happen to us. We'd all talked about it and voted on it as a group. If you two hadn't shown up, we were going to make our move tonight. We all decided it was worth taking the risk. I think that the foster parents had to have been in on this."

Sadie took note of that tidbit of information. The foster home needed to be investigated for links to Igor's network. "Did you have an understanding of who those men were?"

"They talked in Spanish the whole time. Of course they didn't realize that a lot of us knew Spanish. I started learning Spanish in kindergarten. I mean, it's Texas. Anyway, they kept talking thinking that we were just stupid American girls. Little did they know. We were not going to let those guys put us up for sale."

"What did you hear?"

"They worked in the drug business. That was their main focus—lots of talk about various shipments and payments. Money, they were always talking about money. What they were going to be able to sell. They also spoke a lot about a Russian guy named Igor. They hated him. We all thought that Igor had paid them to keep us. I think they wanted the money, but I don't really think they wanted us. They could've hurt us, but those guys never did. We heard them talking, though. They were handing us off to someone else. Getting rid of us. That's why we had to act tonight. Because none of us thought that we would be safe with whoever they were planning to take us to."

Sadie couldn't believe how impressive this girl was. After going through all of this, her voice remained calm and she spoke about the facts without emotion.

"Your mom is going to be so happy to see you."

"I'm going to be grounded forever now. And the worst part is that she's totally right. I should've been more careful. My mom and I do the best we can. She's gone all the time—working and working. Sometimes I just wish she noticed me a bit more. I know she tries her best. But sometimes it's just tough."

"I doubt that you'll be grounded forever. She has to be proud of how you handled yourself. And I think you gave her quite a scare. I wouldn't be surprised if the two of you didn't spend a lot more quality time together after this."

Sadie looked over at Kip. He'd stayed quiet letting her have the conversation with Megan.

"How far are we from the border?" Megan asked.

"A few hours."

"Is it okay if I take a nap?"

"Of course," she said.

"Please wake me up when we're close to home."

Sadie and Kip kept quiet to allow Megan to fall asleep easily. After an hour or so, Kip broke the silence when his phone buzzed. "Can you see what that message says?"

She picked up his phone to read the text message. "The FBI was just checking in. They should be at the border before we get there. Everyone is good."

"That's a huge relief."

"So I guess the drug runners' conscience wasn't as

strong as Jorge had thought. They were still willing to make money from the girls. They just didn't want to have to be the ones in charge of them."

The thought of it made her stomach churn. "That helps our story to Igor."

"Right, you've got a point. So we tell him that by the time we reached the area, the girls were gone. We suspect his hired help double crossed him. He'll be infuriated. And hopefully not direct his anger at us."

"And what do we do when those guys start talking and tell Igor about us?"

"It'll be their word against ours," he said softly. "And we'll have to make sure he believes us."

There was no better feeling than seeing Megan and her mom tightly embrace. The tears that flowed were happy tears from all involved. Megan and her mom had quite a few things to work out, but seeing them together, Kip had no doubts that their relationship would be stronger now.

Kip hadn't felt this good in a long time. He'd been concerned about them being able to save all those girls. It was amazing how things played out. He even considered praying again. He'd take it one step at a time.

Sadie had truly impressed him. She was unlike any woman he'd ever met. So tough and independent yet so caring and understanding. He was drawn to her even though he tried to fight it. He knew he shouldn't, but he couldn't help it and invited Sadie to have dinner. And to his relief and surprise she'd said yes.

Unfortunately, even though they'd saved the girls and Megan was back at home safe, Igor still remained a huge threat. One that couldn't be discounted. There was a lot more to be done if he was to bring down the future leader of the Vladimir network. The FBI was putting the pressure on him to bring them substantial evidence that would hold up in court. Igor needed to be put away for good.

But tonight he didn't want to think about all of that. He just wanted to spend a nice evening with Sadie where they weren't focused on threats or guns or nightmares. He knew it was a bit selfish given the bigger picture, but for one night that's how he wanted to be.

It was far too dangerous to go out when they weren't sure what Igor knew or who he believed. Sadie had suggested that they grill at her place so she could actually spend a little time at home getting ready in case they had to hit the road again. He had picked up some steaks at the store. When he rang her doorbell, he couldn't help but feel a little nervous. Was this a date? Did he want it to be?

She opened the door, and he stood there speechless. She wore a blue sweater dress and strappy sandals. Her long dark hair was flowing down around her shoulders instead of pulled back.

"You look beautiful, Sadie."

"Well, you did say it was a steak dinner. So I figured I could clean up a bit for you." She laughed.

Her two cats rubbed up against his legs, and he reached down and rubbed the black one's furry ears. Even the cats were growing on him. He wondered what Colby would think of them.

"They're really liking you now." She picked up the orange cat in her arms. "I imagine Colby was glad to see you."

"Yup. He had fun at my friend's house. I think he

gets fed extra treats, but when I picked him up his tail looked like it was going to propel him into flight. I couldn't even get upset at his slobbery kisses. I'll have to make sure we go for a good run tomorrow as he seemed to have a lot of pent-up energy."

"I'd like to meet him sometime."

"He'd like you." He smiled. This felt so natural. Everything about Sadie made him smile right now. He truly wasn't used to feeling like this.

"I already made the sides, so all you need to do is fire up the grill."

While he was grilling he wanted to get to know the non-P.I. side of Sadie a bit better. "What was it like growing up in Oregon?"

"Wet and dark." She laughed. "I liked it. We lived in a small town a couple of hours outside Portland. My parents actually had a small farm. I loved riding horses growing up. But I haven't ridden in years. I do miss it."

"You could ride somewhere around here. Plenty of horses. Probably more horses here than in Oregon."

"I'm so busy. I don't have the time. Trying to build my business. It's a lot of work starting a business from the ground up. And at the moment I'm doing it alone with no staff or help. But I wouldn't change it for anything. I love my job."

"You have to have some time for fun."

"Not a lot, lately. I figure I can have fun once I'm more established."

"What about your friends? What do you do with them?"

She looked away and her cheeks flushed. "I don't really have a lot of friends. I tend to not let people get that close. You may have noticed that. Kind of makes it difficult on friendships."

What had happened in her past to make her so guarded? He wanted to ask but didn't want her to start pulling away from him.

"What about you? I know you have your friend that watches Colby. Is he FBI too?"

"No. We're both former military guys. We work out together sometimes."

"Do you think you'll stay with the FBI long-term?"

"You know, I'm not sure. I like it right now. I enjoy the pace. But if I don't stay in the field, I don't know how I'd do sitting behind a desk all the time. Maybe one day I'll want something different."

Satisfied that the steaks were grilled to perfection, he put hers on a plate and then his.

"Go sit at the table, and I'll bring in the rest," she said.

His mouth started watering when he saw the potato salad, green beans and corn bread. He could get used to this.

She sat down at the table. "If I ever decide to expand The Lane Group, you'll be my first call." She reached over and grabbed his hand. "Would you say grace?"

He wasn't expecting that one. Could he do this? Her brown eyes were so sweet and full of hope. He couldn't turn her down. He bowed his head. "Dear Lord. Thank You for this wonderful dinner. And for the amazing company. Thank You for keeping us safe and please continue to watch over us as we work together. Amen."

"Amen," she said. She picked up her fork and knife and started to dig in.

* * *

Guilt started to eat away at Sadie. Kip was slowly opening up to her, and yet she couldn't reveal who she really was to him. She knew she wasn't supposed to disclose her true identity to anyone. Doing so would have huge consequences, and she wasn't sure how Kip would react. But she also realized that going after Igor had ramifications too. Life-changing ones.

They'd done a good job not talking about work tonight, but she knew that was only temporary because Igor called as they were finishing dinner. He wanted another meeting. He wasn't happy about Mexico. He was also pushing for any additional intelligence on Artur. They'd opened that door about his brother, and there was no going back. She worried that Igor may become obsessed over a threat that didn't even exist, and she didn't know whether that would help or hurt her overall mission.

"I should let you get some rest," he said. "I don't have to tell you to lock up and keep your gun within reach."

He took a step closer to her, and she looked into his eyes—his amazingly blue eyes. He reached out and touched her cheek. Just that simple touch melted her heart. He leaned down, and for a moment, she thought he might kiss her. Her heart raced in anticipation. But he whispered in her ear, "I should go."

Disappointed, she just nodded. She was being foolish to think that he'd even want to kiss her. And they had too many other problems to deal with right now.

"One more thing," he said. And then his lips gently brushed hers before he broke away. "Good night, Sadie."

She stood there, dumbfounded. A simple kiss had never been less simple. She reached up and touched her lips. She didn't know how to process this. Her emotions which she normally kept on lockdown now blossomed through her. How could she feel so much from just one kiss? Did he feel it too? Regardless of the kiss there was still a large gulf between them preventing her from truly enjoying the moment. She had to remember she was still on a mission, a very important mission, to stop Igor Vladimir once and for all. Now that Megan was safe, that was exactly what she was going to do. She couldn't let her growing affection for Kip derail her plans.

The next day, Kip was still reeling from kissing Sadie. He knew that he shouldn't have done it. But when he looked down into her perfect brown eyes, he hadn't been able to resist. He'd started to form an attachment to this woman. And that was a very bad idea for a whole host of reasons. Now they were about to go into their meeting with Igor, and he had to keep his head in the game. There was no room for mistakes.

Sadie looked perfectly calm as usual. Today her long hair was pulled back in a low ponytail. She'd acted like the kiss never happened. So far it was business as usual. He wondered how long that would last. In his mind, things had changed, but he didn't know how she felt. He didn't know if he could ever go back to the world he knew before he kissed her.

"You ready for this?" he asked before he pushed the elevator button for the penthouse.

"Yes, I am," she said with a tight smile.

He didn't like her spending more time with Igor. He needed to act like a professional right now. Sadie was capable of taking care of herself. Even though he wanted to be the one protecting her. They needed to have this meeting and push things forward with Igor.

After getting through security, they were shown to Igor's office. The penthouse was everything Sadie had described and more. Lavish was the first word that came to his mind. He'd never be able to live like this. At the end of the day, he was a pretty simple man.

He'd given up his gun to the hired muscle, something he didn't like one bit.

Igor sat at his desk with a frown on his face. "I hear you two had quite a trip to Mexico."

They'd agreed that Sadie would take the lead as she'd have the best shot at managing the situation. "Yes. It wasn't what we were expecting. And it definitely wasn't what I was anticipating based on the conversation we had here before I left. You have serious issues down there, Igor. They need to be addressed." She crossed her arms.

"I'm hearing a lot of different things from many sources across the border." He leaned forward in his chair and looked directly at Sadie—not even giving Kip a glance. "My trusted friend Jorge tells me that the locals have turned against me."

"Based on what we saw, I wholeheartedly agree with his assessment."

She was playing him like a professional. It was almost scary how she didn't flinch under the circumstances. Could she be playing him just like Igor? With that innocent look in her eyes before he kissed her?

Igor nodded and then cocked his head to the side. "The problem is that I'm also hearing that the two of you are the ones who actually disrupted my business down there."

She laughed. A full throated, all out laugh. "That's a good one, Igor. Surely you're not wasting my time with that nonsense." She stood up and straightened her shoulders.

"Sit down, Ms. Lane."

She slowly took her seat but never broke eye contact with Igor.

"I just wanted assurances that we are on the same team here."

"Igor, let's get one thing straight. I'm first and foremost a businesswoman. I came to you wanting to do business. That is still my desire. But I will not have you second-guessing my actions because you're paranoid." She looked over at him. "I want to make things work between us. And I'd like to be fairly compensated for what I'm bringing to the table. That's it."

Igor turned his attention to Kip. "FBI guy, you ought to be glad you have such a strong partner."

"Thank you for the vote of confidence, Igor," she said. "I suggest we move forward with business."

"Perfect," he replied. Then he grinned. "I noticed the FBI tailing me last night. I was a bit disappointed that I spotted them so easily. Did you put the rookie team on me, Kip? Don't I get a little more respect than that?"

"The FBI's incompetence amazes even me. But don't get too lackadaisical. There are still some guys on the team that will not rest until you're put away."

Igor scoffed and leaned back in his chair clasping his arms above his head. "I feel confident that I can deal with FBI surveillance. And for now, I'm going to put a pause on my Mexico operations until I can get a handle on what's going on down there. I don't have the patience to get into the middle of a turf war with the locals, and

I can always find other places in Mexico to do business or move on to another more lucrative opportunity."

"That's probably a smart move," Sadie said.

"Which is why I have another proposition for you two."

"Which is?" she asked with a raised eyebrow.

"I want you to spy on my brother."

"What?" she asked.

"You're the one that planted this seed in my mind, Ms. Lane. So now I want you to do something about it. Bring me actionable information. I want to know if he's really after me—or if he's just trying to get control of the business. I can take some friendly brotherly rivalry. What I cannot stomach is the thought of him selling me out." Igor's eyes darkened.

"Do you know where Artur is now?" Sadie asked.

"He travels a lot. But he lives in New York. I called him just this morning and had a nice talk. I don't want to believe that my only brother is a traitor." He paused. "But I need to know. Do whatever you need to do to get me the answers I seek." He picked up a pen from his desk and scribbled something. Then he handed the piece of paper to Sadie. "That will be your payment if you succeed."

She took the piece of paper from him and looked down at it. "Do we have any restrictions? For example, do you want us to deal directly with him, or only do our work from the distance?"

"I want answers. Any way you have to get them is fine with me. If he is innocent, he will understand."

"And if he's not?" Kip asked.

"I will kill him myself," Igor responded without flinching.

Much to Sadie's credit, she didn't break character. Even when Igor threatened to kill his own flesh and blood.

"I'll keep you updated," she said.

"Yes. No matter how trivial you may think it is. I want to know."

Once they were back in Kip's car, he heard her let out a deep sigh.

"You did great in there," Kip said. "It's a bit eerie that you're able to hide your true emotions so well."

"I've had a lot of practice."

He wondered what she meant by that. "As a P.I.?"

"Yeah," she said quickly. "What in the world are we going to do now? I had no idea he was going to want us to work on this angle. And since we're the ones that made up the story about Artur, we know we're not going to find anything."

"You know, I wouldn't be surprised if Artur does have it out for his older brother. But you're right. This could prove to be difficult. Seems like we're going to have to go on another trip."

"Can we check to make sure he's actually in New York before we go?"

"Yeah."

"And we need to figure out what we're going to do up there."

"I'm going to check in with the field office. There's an agent there who should be able to get me some additional information," he said.

They decided to go to her office and plan their next steps. After some coffee and a snack, they were seated at the table ready to work.

"What was the number Igor wrote down?"

She blew out a breath. “One million.”

“Wow,” he said. “That’s crazy. With family, it’s personal.”

“I know. I wasn’t expecting anywhere near that.” She paused. “What that tells me, is Igor is highly motivated to get to the bottom of this. We can use that to our advantage in gathering evidence against him.”

“Sadie, I should’ve told you this earlier. But now that Megan is safe, we can get you out of this. There’s no reason to put yourself in such personal danger. Even as a consultant for the FBI, we can’t pay you enough to justify those risks.”

She turned toward him. “That decision is mine to make. Do you really think I’d bail now? Do I need to remind you how that meeting just went? If you want to take down the Vladimir network, you need me.”

“There will always be bad men like Igor out there, Sadie. I don’t think I could forgive myself if something happened to you.”

“Nothing is going to happen to me, Kip. I think I’ve shown you that I can hold my own. Against almost anyone.”

“All right,” he said reluctantly.

She stood up and started pacing. “If this is about last night, then let’s talk about that instead.”

“What do you mean?”

“The fact that you kissed me. If you don’t want to work together now because of that, have the courage to say so. Don’t hide behind excuses.”

Ouch, she was really going in for the kill. He shouldn’t have kissed her. Romance always complicated things. Especially working relationships.

“Sadie,” he said as he rose from his chair and walked

to her. "My asking if you wanted out of this operation has nothing to do with my kissing you."

"I find that hard to believe. You're clearly having second thoughts on both."

Without thinking he leaned down and kissed her again. This time he lingered a few moments longer on her sweet lips. Then he pulled back and put his hands on her shoulders. "See, no second thoughts about that, and I think you're an amazing partner. I'm just concerned about your safety."

She looked into his eyes. "I'm sorry, Kip."

"Don't apologize. You're right. You can handle this. I just wanted to make sure you knew that you weren't under any obligations."

"Thanks. I get the risk. And I'm all in."

EIGHT

Kip had kissed her again. Was this really happening? She had been ready to push thoughts that there could be something more with him away when he suggested that she back out of the mission. No way. She was all in just like she said. What she hadn't expected was for him to kiss her a second time once she questioned him about it.

"Do we need to talk about what's going on between us?" she asked. She didn't want to overanalyze things right now, but she also didn't want it to be weird.

"Do you think we do?"

It would be so much easier if she could just tell him the truth. Get it all out there. But she couldn't. Not now. "I just want to make sure that we're comfortable together. This trip to New York could get difficult."

He reached out and grabbed her hand. "Sadie, there are a million different reasons why I probably shouldn't have kissed you the first time and a million more for why I shouldn't have kissed you again. Honestly, it just felt right to me. And I think it feels right to you. But I don't want this to move any more quickly than we're both comfortable with. You're right that we've got a job to do here and that has to be our top priority. But once we've completed the mission, we can talk about whether you'd be interested in seeing me again because I'd like to see you. Does that work?"

She didn't know what to make of his suggestion. Did that mean he wasn't going to kiss her again? "I guess so," she said in a noncommittal fashion. She poured them both more coffee and then took a seat.

"New York," she said.

"Yeah, New York," he replied.

"I think we first have to understand who and what we're dealing with. Once we're clear on that, then we can evaluate whether we can approach him. That's my opinion."

His phone buzzed and he read the text message. "Our FBI guys have eyes on Artur. He is in New York City. Igor wasn't lying. He just had lunch at a swanky place in downtown Manhattan with what my guys describe as a supermodel."

She laughed. "We should book our tickets. And let me call my cat sitter. There's a girl in high school that I use when I have to go out of town. I don't know how long we'll be gone, so I want to make arrangements for Leo and Sammie."

"Good idea. I'll talk to my buddy about Colby."

The next day, they arrived in New York City. Igor had called the night before, ensuring that they would be on a flight out the next day. He'd insisted on booking them first-class tickets and putting them up at a fancy Times Square hotel. The problem was that Igor only booked one room. A very nice suite. Kip, being the gentleman, immediately secured a second room for himself.

As she looked around her plush suite, with a full living room and oversize bedroom, she flopped down on the large bed with a super-soft down comforter. She allowed herself to pretend for just a minute that she had a normal life. That she could actually have a relationship with Kip. That her past wouldn't haunt her daily. But she knew better. She was far from normal. Her baggage was sometimes too much for her even to bear. And she still didn't know how she'd ever tell Kip the truth. No one outside Witness Protection knew who she really was. She had to keep it that way. Her life depended on it. She was already taking a risk by coming to New York, which was a violation of protocol. The problem was that she was in too deep now. The risks of her turning down the trip would be higher than her going. Igor would definitely get suspicious.

She had to fight the desire to kill Igor herself. It would be so easy. One meeting, one shot. It would be all over. She'd found herself praying about it more and more. The temptation was great. Even though she knew it was wrong. Terribly wrong. She'd even dreamed about killing him. Seeking revenge on him for all he'd taken from her. And for getting answers. She desperately wanted to know what the connection had been between her father and Igor.

For now, though, she had to keep with the mission. Kip hadn't kissed her again. That was good and bad. Good because she couldn't see a way forward for them once this was all over. Bad because she had grown to have feelings for him. Feelings she'd never experienced before. At twenty-seven years old, she hadn't dated a lot like most girls her age. She had too many secrets, not to mention plenty of hang-ups. She couldn't deny that she was drawn to Kip. Had the Lord brought him into her life? She needed him and he needed her—though each for very different reasons.

There was a light knock at the door. She opened it without thinking assuming it was Kip. Bad move. The man standing in front of her was not Kip. Definitely not Kip. It was Jay Clifford—the U.S. Marshal who was her Witness Protection contact. He stood there all six foot four, with his fancy suit and perfectly styled dark hair and a scowl on his face. She was in big trouble. She pulled him quickly into her room.

"What are you doing here?"

He walked into her living room and then turned around to face her. "You haven't been returning my check-in calls." Jay kept his voice low. "Then imagine my utter amazement when I find out that you're working with the FBI on the Vladimir case." He crossed his arms over his chest, and he didn't have to say more for her to know he was angry.

"You didn't tell the FBI, did you?"

"Of course not. Some of us know that we shouldn't break protocol. No matter what."

She let out a deep breath. "Thank you."

He took a step toward her. "No, no. You're not off the hook that easy. What is going on?"

"I didn't realize my quest would lead me back to New York."

"You expect me to believe that?"

"It's true. I am working against Igor. I know it doesn't justify my breaking protocol. But I had a client—her daughter was kidnapped by Igor's network. I went to Mexico to rescue her. I started working with the FBI because I was at the wrong place at the wrong time. You know how I feel about them. But now I've gained Igor's trust. I can't just bail. Too much is riding on this. There's more at stake than just my safety. An entire FBI operation and the lives of others matter too."

Jay started pacing back and forth and muttering under his breath. "You know protocol. And you definitely know you're not supposed to be in New York. What were you thinking?"

"I'm in deep cover right now, Jay. I couldn't break it, or I would risk being exposed. And also threatening an FBI investigation."

"How do you know he doesn't recognize you?"

"I know. I can tell. Believe me."

"This is a mess, Sadie. A complete mess." He blew out a breath. "I underestimated your desire for revenge. I foolishly thought you'd moved on and had found an outlet for your anger by being a P.I."

She couldn't help but smile. "That was your first mistake, Jay."

"Hand over your phone. I'm putting a tracker code on it that only I can access. I need to know where you are at all times."

Given the circumstances, she complied.

"Who are you here with?"

"An FBI agent. His name is Kip Moore. We went to Igor as a team. But Igor has taken a liking to me."

"What do you hope to accomplish?"

"Bring Igor to justice for a start."

"You don't need me to tell you how difficult that will be."

"I'm not going to stop trying. You can't pull me off this. Just walk away."

"You could be removed from the program for such a willful violation of protocol."

"Please, I just need time."

"If something happens to you, I'm responsible."

"No. You're not. This is my choice. I can put that in writing if you want," she said with a raised voice.

"Don't you get it, Sadie? You could be killed. I don't have to tell you what type of man Igor is."

"I get it. Believe me. I get it." He was the one who didn't get it.

"Sadie," Kip's voice rang out from behind the door. "Are you okay? Open up."

Oh no. How would she explain Jay being in her room? "You," she said in a hushed tone as she jabbed her finger to his shoulder. "You better think of something fast."

She had no choice but to open the door. Kip stopped short when he saw Jay and pulled his gun.

"Who are you?" he asked, looking to Jay and then back to Sadie.

"I'm an old friend of Sadie's."

Kip's eyes widened in suspicion.

"Yes. This is Jay. I told him I'd be in the city so we could meet up. You can lower your weapon."

Kip narrowed his eyes at Jay and slowly brought down his gun. "All right. Let me know when you're done. So we can get to work."

"No, no. It's fine." Jay shook his head. "We're done catching up for now. It was great to see you, Sadie." Jay gave her a stiff hug and then walked out of the room.

"Wow, well, I don't know what to say." Kip stood with his arms crossed.

She could play this a couple of different ways. Which would be best? "There's nothing to say. He and I are just old friends."

"Didn't look like you two were just friends to me."

"Are you jealous?"

"Of course not," he said. Then he looked at her. "That's a lie. Yeah, I am jealous."

"There's no reason for that. I've known him for many years. He's more like a big brother to me." And that was the truth. She relaxed when she saw his face soften.

"I'm sorry. I can be a total jerk."

She laughed. "Yes you can."

"And since I thought he was your ex, I was prepared to tell you my ex story."

"You can still tell it even though he and I never dated."

"My ex moved on with my fellow ranger team member before she was actually my ex."

"What?" Now, she hadn't expected that.

"Yeah. It's a really ugly story."

"What happened?" She grabbed his hand and led him to the sofa to sit down.

"We were engaged, actually. I thought everything was going great. Man, was I ever wrong." He stopped talking and his shoulders slumped. Then he looked back at her. "During my last deployment, Brad was at home doing some knee rehab. So while I was in the field, putting my life on the line, he made his move on my fiancée, Lacy."

"Whoa. Kip, I'm so sorry." She put her hand on his knee and squeezed.

"Needless to say I was devastated. Not to mention angry with both of them. Brad's betrayal was probably even worse than Lacy's. He was the leader of our team. I lost it and punched him. Hard. Knocked him out."

She couldn't believe this. Seeing the hurt deep in his eyes pained her.

"I knew there was no way I could serve with him again. I decided it was time for a change. I went through a rough patch. I started drinking. A lot. Before I realized it, I was in a downward spiral and I couldn't pull myself out. One night I was sitting at a bar, and the bartender looked at me—the look on his face was full of pity. It was that night I decided I had to get sober—and I haven't had a drink since then. I retired from the military so I wouldn't have to face Brad again and joined the FBI."

It all made so much sense now. His struggle with faith was inextricably tied to what had happened in his past. "It's understandable that you had a severe reaction. You were betrayed—twice. I don't know who this Brad guy is, but he clearly was in the wrong. But that doesn't mean that God's plan for you isn't being played out. Don't let your anger toward Brad continue to hurt your relationship with God."

"I know you're right, but it's much harder to come to grips with than you might think. I kept asking God, why me? I wallowed in self-pity. That was part of what led to the drinking problem. And when I drank, I only felt numb. I knew it wasn't the way to deal with my problems, but I felt weak—out of control. A stronger man would have turned to his faith. But I wasn't strong, Sadie. I turned away from God and everything I'd ever believed in. It took a toll on me."

She held his hand and rested her head on his shoulder. What really hurt her was knowing how devastated he would be if he knew that she hadn't told him about her past. But what choice did she have? She had none.

Jay's visit just reminded her how much her life hung on the thread of keeping her identity a secret.

She lifted up her head and looked at him. "God is patient, Kip. He understands your pain. He hasn't abandoned you. I promise."

"I know that now. You've been a blessing to me, Sadie. I can't help but think that us getting to know each other has been part of God's plan to try and bring me back to where I need to be. I'm not going to lie and say I'm there yet. Because I'm just not. But I want to be. And having your friendship and support has been a huge boost. I never want to go back to that darkest of dark places ever again."

"You don't have to."

"And to top it all off, I still feel guilt about what happened in Iraq during my last deployment with Brad. The nightmares I have are about Iraq, not about the cheating. I think I hold Brad responsible. And I hold myself responsible. I can't help but to think that I could've done more to save innocent lives. A village was being attacked by militants, and we were told to retreat because it was too risky of an operation for us. But I knew that we could have done more to help save the inhabitants. Because we didn't act, the entire village was slaughtered."

"Look at me, Kip." She placed her hands on his face. "You're not the one who killed those innocent people. It sounds to me as if had you tried to do something, you could've been killed, too. Just think of all the lives you saved in Iraq. Guilt will eat you from the inside out. You can't let it do that." She rested her head on his shoulder again.

That sat quietly on the couch for a few minutes. Then

he was the one to break the silence. "We should talk about what our first move is."

She lifted her head from his shoulder and made eye contact. "Shouldn't we put eyes on him? Get an idea whether he has a routine in place."

"I spoke with our New York field office. They've got a huge file on him. He works in an office building near Times Square. But from what I'm hearing he doesn't actually work that much. He's a real playboy. Always wining and dining with the ladies."

"Great," she said, sarcastically.

"He has his favorite restaurants. And he drops by his casino on occasion in Atlantic City."

"Seems like he has it really tough. Doesn't look like he'll be taking over the family business with that cavalier lifestyle. Makes me wonder if he even wants the job."

"Don't be fooled by his antics. He's power hungry. And intensely competitive with his brother. He still takes his father to dinner once a week. He's not stupid. He's just playing a different game than Igor."

"Making him no less dangerous than his brother."

"Exactly. Just with a prettier face and a flashier manner." He sighed. "The FBI is having an awful time getting any evidence against him. We thought about sending in one of our guys undercover, but no one thought they could pull it off."

"He'll slip up. All criminals do eventually."

"Yeah. The FBI has a bigger beef with Igor. There's no evidence tying Artur to any human trafficking. The whole network needs to be brought down, but Igor is our top priority. I don't believe he's going to quit his trafficking operation. He just needs to readjust his business strategy to make sure he's paying off the right drug lords in Mexico."

"Another reason we need to stop him. But I don't think we want Igor to kill Artur. And if we bring Igor evidence of Artur working with the FBI, that's exactly what will happen. I have no doubt about that."

"Yes. But how do we provide proof that Artur is not cooperating with the FBI? We're the ones that came up with the story to begin with."

"If we can say that we've had him under surveillance and can account for all of his meetings, I think that might at least satisfy Igor for the short term."

"You ready to explore the city?"

"Yes." Kip looked down at his watch. "Artur should be coming out of the office building within the hour. So we should get in place."

"Have you been here before?"

"A few times. But I'm not totally familiar with the city. How about you?"

"Same." And that was true. This is where she was born, but she only lived in New York for the first eight years of her life. Once she went into Witness Protection, she'd been sent to Oregon—basically the farthest location she could get from New York and stay within the continental United States. She didn't have many specific memories of the city at all. And New York was one place she had been forbidden to visit.

She didn't enjoy all of the crowds of people and the hustle and bustle. El Paso was much more her speed. However, it would be easy to blend into the New York crowds. But she couldn't help the feeling that if someone wanted to find her, that she wouldn't be safe anywhere.

"Just a few more blocks," Kip said.

While not as hot as Texas, the New York sun was still strong, and Sadie felt sweat bead on her brow. For some reason, Kip had set a very fast pace as they walked down the bustling city streets.

"You're practically jogging," she said, trying to keep up.

He slowed down. "Sorry, I think I got a burst of adrenaline and wasn't thinking that we have plenty of time." He laughed.

"This is perfect," he said, pointing. "We can sit at that bench over there. We'll have eyes on the main exit."

"There will be a lot of people exiting this building. We'll need to make sure we don't lose him in the crowd."

They waited for what seemed like an eternity. She watched closely as person after person left the building—most dressed in suits, carrying briefcases. All seeming as if they were in a hurry. This was the New York lifestyle she'd heard so much about. Is this how she would've become if her parents had lived? What career field would she have chosen? Perhaps she would have been an accountant or lawyer. Living in the big city, in a small but trendy apartment? It made her wonder. Would she have been happy, normal and well-adjusted?

"There he is," Kip said, breaking her out of her thoughts.

He grabbed her hand, and she knew they were going to follow Artur. Artur didn't look anything like she expected. He hadn't been in the courtroom years ago. He'd been too young. He didn't resemble Igor at all as he had much darker features. He was a bit taller and more muscular—he probably hit the gym a lot. That was consistent with his lifestyle. His brown hair was cut short and neatly styled. His dark designer suit probably cost a month's worth of her regular P.I. salary. He walked briskly with his head held high—seemingly oblivious to everyone else around him. Unlike Igor, he did not travel with a security entourage on a regular basis. She wished she could get inside his head. He seemed so different than his brother. She wasn't so foolish as to think he was one of the good guys, but he had to be better than Igor.

"Where do you think he's headed?" she asked.

"You're not going to believe this," Kip said, squeezing her hand. "He's walking straight toward a Broadway theater."

"He's going to see a show?" Just when she thought things were already strange. Now they were even stranger.

"Maybe."

"We'll lose him in the crowd."

"We're not going to go in," Kip said. "But focus on the exits. If he leaves we'll tail him."

"I'm guessing he's using this as a diversion. Do you think he's paranoid?"

Kip laughed. "It really isn't paranoia. We're following him, right?"

"Yeah."

They stood outside the building in front of the main exit.

"One of us should go to the rear exit," he said.

"I'll go."

"Are you sure?"

"Yes. I'm ready for this. I'll text you if he comes out. You do the same."

Sadie was grateful to have a few minutes alone to

collect her thoughts. Her moment of respite didn't last long. Artur stepped out of the rear exit. He looked back over this shoulder and started walking.

"I've got you," she whispered. Adrenaline coursed through her veins. This was the type of assignment she was made for and excelled in. Perfect for a P.I. Get the information but be invisible. She hung back long enough to put some space between her and Artur. She fired off a text to Kip. Then she made her move.

She headed briskly down the street, making sure not to lose him. He was headed west toward a construction area. He walked around the corner and into the narrow alley. She paused again and then followed. The alley was dark. In all black, she blended right into the darkness. Artur was up ahead, leaning against the side of the building. A man was approaching him. Artur didn't seem concerned. That must have meant he knew him.

She had to get a bit closer. She needed to know what they were saying. No sign of Kip. She took a few steps, not making even the slightest noise. The two men appeared to be focused on each other and were oblivious to what was going on around them. It was clear to Sadie that they thought they were totally alone. She walked a couple more steps then crouched down behind a smelly Dumpster. Now she was close enough to hear the conversation.

"You've got problems," the man said to Artur.

"Don't I always," Artur replied. "Tell me. What did my loving brother do now?"

"His operation down in Mexico has garnered a lot of attention. My guys were upset that you didn't give us the heads-up on what was going on down there. Human trafficking? Running against the local drug lords? Our people are getting antsy. They're concerned you're holding back on us. Remember we have a deal. You have to follow through, though, or there is no deal."

"I know we have a deal. You have to understand, my brother doesn't exactly trust me right now. He's trying to succeed our father. He's not going to be giving me all the operational details on his ventures—I'm the competition."

The man poked a finger into Artur's shoulder. "Our deal was clear. You help us bring him down, you get complete immunity. Every other government agency is investigating the whole family's operation. We can protect you, but only if you get us something we can work with. It has to be airtight. You know what our top priority is."

"And why should I trust the DEA? I hear that the FBI is now running the show."

The man shook his head. "No. The FBI is focusing on the trafficking angle. We have the power, authority and ultimate jurisdiction here as far as you're concerned. You have to help us put an end to your brother's drug business, and that's what we need to focus on. Rest assured the FBI and plenty of other government agencies will deal with the rest."

"So what are my options?" Artur asked.

"We need evidence. Concrete evidence of your brother's drug business, especially the cross-border operations. We have to have something that can stand up in federal court. I know you've refused to wear a wire in your face-to-face meetings. But I seriously urge you to reconsider. Once this offer is off the table, you're on your own. And I can't do a thing to stop anyone else from coming after you—including your brother. Work with us and I can guarantee your safety."

"You know if I wear a wire, I might as well sign my own death warrant."

The man laughed. "Artur, I think that's already been signed. Once your brother finds out you made the first deal with us, it's all over. You'll be dead to your brother. To your whole family. The only way out is to cooperate fully with us, and we will then help you."

"What do you think I've been doing?"

"I don't know because when I get additional reporting from other sources that you haven't provided me, it starts making me get a bit nervous about you. I wonder why you even started working with us to begin with."

"It was the right thing to do," Artur said softly.

"Yes. You're the Vladimir brother with a conscience. We recognize that. But now's not the time to get nostalgic over family ties. I have a job to do and so do you. You can turn around your family businesses and make sure they are all of the legal variety once Igor is locked up. In the meantime, we need that evidence. And we need it now."

"I'll get back to you soon."

Sadie tried desperately to process what she had just heard. Artur turned around and started walking back in the direction of the theater. She stayed low and out of sight. Just as she was about to stand up, she felt a hand on her shoulder.

NINE

Kip pulled Sadie to her feet. He couldn't believe this. The DEA was running an entirely different investigation—and had been doing it for some time now based on what he'd heard. As he and Sadie walked back to their hotel, he felt a bit in the dark. The DEA had to have very good reasons for not informing his FBI team of their specific investigation with Artur. Must mean that they had something big—even bigger than what the FBI had. Cross-border drug smuggling was huge. And the funds from that business directly aided the trafficking network. This was all part of the governmental maze of putting away the bad guys.

He looked over at Sadie. This had been a surprise to them both. He could tell that the wheels were turning in that head of hers. She was smart, and she wanted to understand all the dynamics at play. Well, he could tell her one thing she already knew: this operation just got a lot more complicated.

They went to her room since, thanks to Igor, she had a suite with the large living room.

"Where do we even begin?" she asked as she made some coffee. He took a moment to compose his thoughts. He didn't want to take his anger and frustration out on Sadie. She didn't deserve that.

"You're upset that you weren't fully in the know," she said.

He started to talk and she held up her hand. "Don't even deny it. I get it. Let's talk it through. First, why don't you tell me what you heard? I'll let you know if I heard anything more or different."

She poured him some coffee. He took a sip and looked at her. "I heard this." He paused and leaned toward her. "The DEA has made a deal with Artur. Artur brings them concrete evidence that could hold up in court against Igor, and then Artur is a free man." He took a deep breath. "And, of course, the DEA has been conducting their sting operation unbeknownst to the FBI."

She took a sip of coffee. "They want Artur to wear a wire to get Igor to provide specific information on his human-trafficking operation. He's reluctant. The DEA cares about the connection to the drug business," she said matter-of-factly.

"This is tricky. Both organizations think they are taking the lead. The real question is—who is actually in charge? The FBI believes this is their investigation. Our investigation. They're operating as if it is. The FBI thinks the DEA is merely playing a supportive role, and only as needed, for the drug angle."

"Where does that leave you?" she asked.

"I really have no clue," he replied softly. "I don't know what the right thing to do here is."

"If the DEA is actually in charge, and running a secret investigation, you wouldn't want to blow that cover

over some inter-agency issues. Even if you have issues with how it all went down."

He knew she was right, as much as it pained him to acknowledge her assertion.

"And this is even more reason why we can't let anything happen to Artur. We need something to take back to Igor to help prove his innocence. Which is a problem since we're the ones who said he was guilty."

"See, this is why agencies need to talk." He sighed and ran his hand through his hair. "If I'd been in the loop, we would have never put the idea in Igor's head that there was an issue of loyalty with Artur. We've put him in danger—the DEA's star witness has a bull's eye on his back. Thanks to us, Igor could try to kill his brother."

She flinched. He wondered what he'd said to bother her.

"And we thought we had problems before," she said. He watched her as she twirled her hair and tied it up in a knot. In the midst of all of this, he still couldn't deny his ever-growing attraction to her.

"But we'll get through this," she said. "Together." She reached out and grabbed his hand. He couldn't help himself. He leaned closer to her and pressed his lips gently to hers, his hand cradling her face. They really were a team.

He pulled back, and they sat in silence. But not an awkward silence. A silence that he could see himself wanting on a Saturday afternoon. Just the two of them enjoying each other's company. At what point had he fallen for her? He knew it couldn't work—wouldn't work in the long-term—but he was going to enjoy her company while it lasted.

"The question now is, how do we help Artur?" Sadie asked. "The game has changed. He's no longer a totally guilty party like Igor. He's working with the DEA, so we need to make this right."

"If we don't report back in to Igor, he's going to be suspicious. That is if he's not already. I have a bad feeling about the risks here."

"I'll send him an update that we tracked Artur to a Broadway show. I won't mention that we saw him leave. Hopefully, this will quench his thirst for immediate information. But we're going to have to figure out what to do next. Do you actually think Artur is trying to do the right thing?"

"Or do I think he's trying to save himself?" he asked.

"Right."

"You know, I'm not sure. It's possible that he really does have some good in him, and that he wants to do what's right. But on the other hand, he could just be looking out for himself. Don't forget he runs a big part of the Vladimir drug-business. So an immunity deal would look very attractive. If it's between him and Igor, I'd say he's going to look out for number one."

"Yeah. Maybe it's too much to hope that one person in the family isn't evil."

"I wonder how long the DEA has been working with him?" he asked more to himself than to Sadie. "The wire part was interesting."

"Why not just do it? Wouldn't that be the easiest way to get the evidence?"

"Because if something went wrong, then Artur would be toast. And he knows that. He's smarter than anyone probably gives him credit for."

She looked beautiful, but he could also see that this

was starting to wear on her. There was a touch of dark circles forming under her eyes. He had to remind himself that they'd been through a lot in the past few days. "Why don't we call it a night?"

"You sure?" she asked.

"Yeah. I know I'm tired." He was tired. And he thought if he admitted it, she might be more willing to get some much needed rest. "I'm right next door if you need me."

"Good night, Kip," she said.

He thought about kissing her again. He really wanted to. But thought better of it. He needed to make sure he was a gentleman.

Sadie's phone kept buzzing. Who in the world would be calling her in the middle of the night? She looked at the hotel clock on her nightstand and it showed three thirty. She groaned. If Kip needed something, he would've just knocked on her door.

She picked up her phone and saw the number that she was familiar with. No name associated with it, but she knew it was Jay. What did he want now? A sense of dread washed over her.

"Yes," she picked up the phone.

"We've got an issue. A big problem."

"What's wrong?" She sat up in the bed. Jay was never one to dramatize a situation. If he said they had a big problem, what that actually meant was they had a huge problem.

"Someone from the FBI hacked into your sealed file."

"What? Who?"

"I don't know, but I had one of our consulting technical experts trace the IP address back to the FBI field office in El Paso. And whoever it was has stellar computer skills. It would take someone at the highest level of hacking ability to crack into a Witness Protection file."

Her mind raced. It couldn't have been Kip. He was in New York with her. But someone in the FBI field office knew the truth. She shivered. "How is that even possible?"

"They were able to get past the initial firewalls because of their other clearances. But the fact that they got in there in the first place made me think they were suspicious of you. It's not something you just happen upon. You have to be looking for it. Maybe they ran a background check on you. When they weren't satisfied, they started poking around."

"What do we do now?"

"I'm hoping and praying that since this is FBI, that you will be safe. But I have a sinking feeling about this. We have to assume the worst. And the worst is that this is connected to Igor somehow. I certainly don't believe in coincidences. It would be foolish to do so in my line of work. You know my motto—Trust No One."

He'd drilled it into her head when he'd been assigned as her contact five years ago. "Don't go back to El Paso. Stay put in New York, but I don't want you in that hotel anymore. You need to get out in the morning. Go to populated areas where you can blend in, like stores or museums. I'm going to do some more digging, and I'll let you know as soon as I figure out the next move. Sadie, I hate to say this, but this is the exact reason why you never should've gotten involved in this investigation in the first place."

The last thing she wanted right now was a lecture. "Call me when you know more."

She hung up and lay back down. This was not good. Assuming the FBI agent who looked into her past was one of the good guys, he would be bound to report to Kip what he found out. *Lord, what should I do?* she prayed. She knew that her past was going to come back to haunt her at some point, but she wasn't ready to deal with it now. Could she just pretend like all was fine tomorrow until she heard more from Jay? She would have to make sure she followed Jay's directions on where she could go. How would she explain that to Kip?

Morning came, and she'd had a fitful rest of the night. By the time she'd showered and gotten dressed, she felt a little better. But still on edge. She ordered breakfast up to the room and invited Kip to join her. He looked well-rested and very handsome. She was scared that she looked a bit frightful. If she did, he knew better than to mention it.

"What are we going to do all day while Artur is at the office?" she asked. "I don't want to sit around the hotel."

"I thought we might explore the city a bit."

"All right." She was relieved he suggested that after hearing Jay's directive to stay in populated areas.

She felt awful. When Kip found out the truth about her, he'd see her just like he saw his ex-fiancée and Brad. It killed her to think about it. She knew she didn't have much more time with him before her cover was completely blown.

"Any ideas?" he asked.

"I don't suppose you're into museums?" Metal detectors would help keep guns away.

"What?" he asked mockingly. "Do I seem that uncultured to you?"

"I didn't mean it that way. Just that most guys aren't really into that stuff."

"Truthfully, art isn't my thing."

"What about natural history? I'd love to go to that museum."

"Dinosaurs are very manly. That I can handle."

She thought the museum would satisfy Kip's urge to go out, and provide some level of safety. Given what Jay had told her, she didn't want to be out in the open. She preferred crowded areas, where it would be easier to blend in or shake a tail. She'd text Jay where they were going just in case.

They walked out of the hotel and into the busy New York City streets. He grabbed her hand. "We'll need to get on the subway."

"Guess you can't be in New York and not go on the subway." As soon as she stepped out of the hotel, she felt goose bumps on her arms. It definitely wasn't cold. She couldn't help the feeling that someone was watching her. She turned around quickly and saw tons of people bustling down the street. There was no way she could spot a threat right now. Which would mean it would be difficult for anyone to find her, too. She felt overwhelmed.

The nearest stop was just a few blocks from their hotel. They read the map and figured out what direction they needed to go to get to the American Museum of Natural History. The subway was full of people. She cringed as she saw a furry rat run by on the tracks. This was it. This really was New York.

She felt her heartbeat speeding up, but she was trying to play cool. When someone bumped into her arm, she instinctively went for her weapon. The weapon she didn't have. Then she realized that there was no threat. Just a teenager not looking where he was going.

They stood up in the crowded subway car until they arrived at their stop and it was time to exit. She'd suggested the museum before she had fully thought it through. But it seemed like the best alternative. Jay had told her they couldn't stay in the hotel. If Igor was on to them, he would know exactly where they were if they stayed. She wished that things were different, and that she could tell Kip what was going on. Inform him of the very real threat. Someone knew her real identity. Someone knew about Lydia.

Pushing those thoughts out of her mind, she tried to focus on Kip. He looked over and smiled at her. She loved museums—especially ones that had planetariums. A childhood memory flashed through her mind. Her father taking her to the planetarium when she was in first grade. He was one of the lead parents on the field trip. Since he was a scientist, he'd loved every minute of it. Her heart broke reliving the loss. And the still unanswered questions about what her father could've been involved with that led to his death and the death of her mother.

"What're you thinking about?" he asked.

"Everything I want to see here. I'd love to see a show at the planetarium. What do you think?"

"As long as I get to see the dinosaurs. That's my only request."

They walked up the many steps into the museum and stood in line to buy tickets. The first stop was getting tickets to the planetarium. A tall man with a baseball hat stood by the entrance. He made eye contact, and a shot of fear went through her. When she looked back over toward him, he was gone. Trying to shake it off, she focused her attention back on Kip.

She had no idea what they were showing, but she didn't care. The dark room would provide her with some level of comfort. It wasn't like the enemy was just going to pop up in the seat next to her.

"Let's do the planetarium show first. Then we'll see whatever you want."

He grabbed her hand into his own and it felt so natural. Like they were on a real date. Unfortunately, nothing about this was a regular date. When Kip found out the truth, he'd never speak to her again. She so didn't want to be the one to cause him pain. Not after he'd told her everything he'd been through. But she wasn't sure there was any way to prevent it.

They walked into the planetarium and took their seats. As they waited for the show to begin, her heart was heavy. Why couldn't she share just a little bit about her past with Kip?

"Kip," she said.

"Yes." He looked over at her. His eyes were as blue as the ocean.

"There's a lot from my past that you don't know about me."

"We all have issues in our past, Sadie. You're the one who told me that's it's important to move forward."

She nodded. "I know, but I'd still like to talk to you about some of it. Soon." She couldn't do it now. While it would be much easier to blurt out her biggest secret, something held her back.

"The show's about to start. But any time you want to talk just let me know."

The show was about stars, and she settled in as the narrator's smooth voice began. Kip held her hand throughout. A simple sign of affection that warmed her heart. She took it all in and enjoyed the presentation. With the darkness surrounding them, she wished she could take Kip and disappear to a faraway place. Somewhere away from all of the violence and pain that surrounded them both—in their past and in their present.

When it was over, she dreaded the lights coming back on. It meant back to reality. And back to the threats. She looked over at Kip, and he was all smiles. How she wanted so badly to confide in him. He'd be her support system. But it wasn't possible now. She forced a grin, and they walked out together.

Glancing over her shoulder, she thought she saw the same man with a baseball hat pulled down low. But she could tell he was staring at her. Was it just her imagination? She couldn't take the risk. They needed to get out of this area and lose this guy. She grabbed Kip's hand and practically dragged him away. "Now you get your dinosaurs. As much as you want."

They found the dinosaur area, and she marveled at Kip's sincere interest. He was really into it. Much more than she ever expected.

"When I was little, I used to be dinosaur crazy," he said. "They still fascinate me. Even after all these years."

He looked stuck in his thoughts staring at the huge T. rex that was the focal point of the room. She decided to let him take it in, and she wandered the room looking for the mysterious man in the hat. She was on high alert.

A hand touched her shoulder. She spun around and standing there was Jay.

"What're you doing here?" she asked.

He grabbed her arm. "You have to come with me."

"No. I can't just leave Kip."

His grip tightened. "You can and you will, Sadie. You're in real danger. I'll explain once we're out of here. I have to get you to safety. Now."

She stole a glance back over at Kip—still standing by the T. rex. She couldn't believe she was about to do this. But in the end, she knew she had to. It was better this way. Conversations, sad goodbyes and recriminations would be too much for both of them.

"He'll think something has happened to me."

"He'll know the truth soon enough." He tugged firmly on her arm. "We have to go. I'm sorry. There's no more time to argue about this."

She didn't want to leave him. What would he think?

Then she heard a rapid succession of gunshots that sounded like they came from right outside. The next thing she knew she was facedown on the ground with Jay on top of her back.

"Are you okay?" he asked with ragged breath.

"Yes. I'm not hit. Are you?"

"No. We've gotta move now."

"Sadie!" Kip yelled.

Mass chaos ensued as museum patrons fled the room. People were screaming and grabbing their children in their arms. She looked around for the man in the hat but didn't see him.

Kip ran over to her and Jay. Kip pulled her up off the floor.

A flash of recognition sparked in Kip's eyes. "You," he said.

"We've got to get out of here now," Jay barked at them both.

"But..." Kip said.

Sadie grabbed on to Kip's arm. "Listen to him. I'll explain everything when we get out of here. I promise you that." Police sirens were already blaring. If they didn't get out soon, the entire place would be on lock-down.

They made a run for the emergency exit and pushed through it. The hot air hitting her face. Her feet pounded against the pavement as she ran a block or two with Kip and Jay right behind her. The hammering of her heart radiated through her body. Jay stopped her and hailed a cab. Jumping in the cab first, she let out a breath. Jay hopped in the front seat and gave the cabbie an address and signaled to her and Kip not to talk yet. Things had escalated, that's for sure. Jay wouldn't just grab her like this if it hadn't. Had he known the shooter was there? Was it the man in the hat?

The cab dropped them off at a hotel parking garage. Sadie wasn't quite sure what was next.

"I've got a car in the garage." He guided them through the ground floor to the elevator. He pushed Six, and they rode up. Her heart pounded. She needed answers. She needed information. What had happened? And how in the world was she going to make Kip understand?

Sensing her apprehension, Jay touched her arm. "I'll explain everything in the car."

Kip shot him a look.

She nodded and Jay stuck right beside them as they

walked through the rows of cars to a nondescript midsize gray vehicle. He crouched down and checked under the car, which was one of the first major signs that this was even more serious than she had expected.

"Get in," he said as he opened the passenger door for her. He pulled a bag out of the backseat and gave it to her. "There's a wig in there and glasses. Please go ahead and put them on. Kip, you take the backseat."

She opened the bag as he started the car. Sure enough, there was a curly blond wig and a pair of designer sunglasses. Whipping her hair back into a bun, she put on the wig as he had instructed.

Once they were out of the garage, she looked over at Jay who had his eyes on the road and a tight grip on the wheel.

"Wait a minute," Kip said, leaning up to the center console. "I see some silent communication between the two of you. What's going on?"

"Can I?" she asked Jay.

"Under the circumstances, we have no choice."

Sadie turned around facing the backseat and felt tears well up in her eyes. "Kip, I haven't been completely honest with you."

"About what?"

She took a deep breath and prayed that she'd be able to do this. *Hold it together,* she told herself. "I'm in Witness Protection."

"You're what?"

"Sadie has been in Witness Protection since she was eight years old," Jay added.

"Why? What happened?"

Here it goes. "I was born Lydia Mars. And I was Lydia for only eight years. Until the day that Igor Vladimir walked into my house and shot my parents. I saw him pull the trigger."

His blue eyes widened in disbelief.

"I'm so sorry I couldn't tell you. I haven't ever told anyone, given the protocol. But things have changed."

"And I hate to bring more bad news to the situation," Jay said. She watched as his grip on the wheel tightened, and he glanced over at her. "He knows about you."

"Who knows?" she asked but already knew the answer.

"Igor."

"How?" She had to force herself to breathe. Panic squeezed at her heart. Now was not the time for an anxiety attack. She had to focus. Too much was riding on this.

"That FBI agent I told you about. The one who tapped into your files. He's dirty. He flipped for fifty grand."

"What agent?" Kip asked.

"My sources tell me that Igor started getting increasingly paranoid. Another call came in from Mexico late last night, and one of the guys swore to him that you two were the ones who busted out the girls. Apparently, he was already getting suspicious of you, Kip, because he put some feelers out at the FBI to recruit someone into his camp. When the price was right, he found a dirty agent—a guy by the name of David Berkowski who has been digging around. Once Berkowski had the money wired to him first thing this morning, he sold Kip out. Told Igor all about the FBI's investigation and how Kip was undercover. Of course, Igor went ballistic. Then Berkowski told Igor about you, Sadie. He used that piece of information to try to get Igor to give him more money."

"How do you know all of this?" she asked.

"Someone else at the FBI had started growing suspicious of Berkowski before this even happened. He had been acting strange, and it raised some red flags with some more seasoned members of the team. Turns out he had a gambling problem and really needed money. They tapped his phone. So we have the whole conversation between him and Igor on tape. And that's what did it. He's put out a million-dollar bounty on you, Sadie."

"Whoa." The thudding of her heart was almost too much to bear. She was good as dead. "What did Igor say to Berkowski about me?"

"You can imagine that he was very upset about being duped. He'd assumed that you were long out of the picture, given your young age when you testified. He clearly hadn't forgotten you, but maybe you weren't in the forefront of his mind, since you'd stuck with the program so closely. That is up until now."

"And what about Kip?"

"I'm sure the FBI is going to want to take action on this. They would normally take you into protective custody, Kip, since Igor's put a bounty out on you. But now you're with us. We have to stick together. The shooter outside the museum was probably one of Igor's thugs."

"I can't believe this is happening," she said softly. Her worst nightmares were coming true. And now she'd put the man she'd fallen in love with in danger. Wait. Love? Yes, that had to be what it was. She couldn't let him die because of her. Tears fell down her cheek. Kip would probably never forgive her. He sat silently in the backseat.

"Keep it together, Sadie." Jay looked at her for a second before turning his attention back to the road. "I'll get you two set up somewhere safe where Igor will not be able to find you. Then we can plan the next move from there. I'm not going to let Igor get to you. I promise. Take a few deep breaths. We'll work through this. I totally understand that right now things seem dire. And they are. You know I've never lied to you over the years. Igor and his network have a far reach. But I'll get you to safety, and we'll figure it out."

"What about Berkowski? Has the FBI taken him into custody?" Kip asked.

Jay paused before responding. "They didn't get a chance. I just learned that Igor had him killed. Time of death within the last two hours."

"Oh no. We have to stop this monster. Before he kills again." She closed her eyes and started praying. Because right now God was her only hope.

After a few minutes of prayer, she tried to compose herself. "Where are we going?"

"Away."

"C'mon, Jay. You've got to give me more than that."

"We've got a plane waiting. Honestly, I'm not sure of the exact destination. Everything right now is so tightly guarded. On a need-to-know basis—and then even a need-to-know-at-the-time. I'll get the flight manifest once we arrive."

A plane. She hated flying. But she didn't have a choice. She had to get as far away from where Igor thought she was as quickly as possible. But she couldn't escape the haunting feeling that wherever she went, he wouldn't be far behind.

TEN

Sadie buckled herself into the seat of the small airplane and tried to brush aside the inkling of claustrophobia that was descending on her.

"You okay?" Jay asked from the seat directly across from her. Aside from the pilot, the plane only had room for a few additional passengers. Kip sat beside her.

"I just don't like flying."

"Just remember to breathe. And you'll be fine."

"Where are we going?" Kip asked.

"We're headed to Colorado."

She put her head in her hands and said a prayer. She needed strength right now. For that matter, she always needed strength. Her world, or rather the world that she and the Witness Protection Program had carefully crafted, was crashing down around her. She couldn't blame Kip if he hated her. She'd been the one to talk about faith and honesty, and look how that had turned out. Deep down she knew that she did the right thing by not telling him who she was. But she felt she did the wrong thing by allowing herself to form a real connection with him. She could tell he had feelings for her too. And that's where she was in error. She prayed for forgiveness, for guidance and for the capability to get through this.

Jay leaned forward. "If it makes you feel any better, the flight will be broken up. We'll stop in a couple of hours to change planes. Just an extra security precaution."

"Do we know where Igor is right now?" she asked.

"No, he was last spotted in El Paso yesterday morning. But with his private jet, he has mobility that is hard to track. Although, he isn't the one that I'm concerned about. I'm more interested in his hired guns."

"What else do you know about the investigations?"

"I know about the FBI investigation. Is there something else?"

So he didn't know about the DEA. Or if he did, he was playing dumb. Should she tell him? She looked over at Kip who shrugged his shoulders—he was obviously frustrated. It was her call to make. "We tracked Artur in New York to a meeting he had with a DEA agent. The DEA is also investigating the Vladimir network."

"I can't say I'm surprised. The drug-trafficking part of their business is growing exponentially. That's something the DEA would want to be a part of."

"Are they doing an inquiry to make sure Berkowski was the only mole?" she asked.

"I'm sure they are. But my sole focus is the safety of my witness. Which means you. What the FBI or the DEA does is their business. You're my witness. And I've never lost a witness. You understand that?"

"I appreciate it. I know you're upset with me."

"You were doing so well. You had been following the rules completely. For years. I know your file by heart. I actually didn't have any doubts that you'd stick with the program forever. I see I underestimated your desire to seek revenge on Igor. I should've known better. When I heard that Igor was expanding his operations into Texas, I should've gone to you directly. But I thought you were doing so well, I didn't want to cause problems. I was wrong about that and will probably face a disciplinary hearing. No going back now, though. We have to move forward and do what is best for you. And the top priority in all of that is keeping you safe. I'm hoping that the FBI investigation will yield something to nail Igor once and for all. He deserves to be in jail for the rest of his life."

Once they were airborne, the plane bumped up and down, driving her crazy. She knew the turbulence would be rough in the small plane.

"Do you get motion sickness?" Kip asked. It was the first thing he'd said to her directly.

"No. I just don't like flying. Hopefully I won't get ill." Although as she said it, she wondered if she might. Her stomach rumbled, gripped by a wave of nausea. She'd been through a lot. The mental and emotional strain bore down on her.

She looked at Kip and knew he was mad at her. She'd not been honest. Hadn't he had enough pain and betrayal in his life already? It hurt her to think that he might believe she was just using him to further her own personal battles. How could she ever make him understand?

At the beginning, she certainly was willing to work with him because it helped her get to Igor. After all, he was the one who brought her the consulting offer. But she took it. And they'd saved those innocent girls in the process. That was one positive. However, somewhere along the way, Kip became something more to her. He definitely broke the FBI mold that had haunted her for so many years. He was a good man. He deserved better than this. Especially given what he'd been through. Would it ever be possible to make it up to him? To make him understand what Igor had taken from her?

And her poor father. She knew it was useless to continuously rack her brain in search of explanations. Igor might be the only person who could tell her truly why he came after her family. She wanted to get that chance to confront him. In some ways, she wished she'd taken the opportunity when she'd had it. She'd learned that the FBI agent that failed to protect her family had died in a car accident years later. So, she could never go to him for answers.

They had been just an average middle-class family living in New York City. What had her father done? Or seen? Something that made eighteen-year-old Igor come to their home and shoot both her parents. In the back of her mind, she worried that her father might have been involved with something illegal. He seemed like such a nice and normal man. But that was to an eight year old. Could he have been wrapped up in the Vladimir network? Did he have a history with Igor's father, Sergei?

One thing was certain: she was going to do everything in her power to find answers. Jay might think his biggest job was keeping her safe. He was wrong. His biggest job would be to keep her from escaping. Because she was going on a manhunt for Igor Vladimir.

"Kip, can we talk?"

"I'm not ready to talk about this yet, Sadie. I'm sorry."

And her heart broke in two.

* * *

By the time they'd changed planes and made it to Colorado, Sadie's legs were cramping and her head ached. The second leg of the flight was even worse, especially as they descended down through the mountains. Kip was still giving her the silent treatment. She couldn't blame him. He would probably need a bit of time to process all of this. And right now everyone was tense and on edge. Sadie was gripped by fear of what was to come.

They'd driven in silence to a cabin in the mountains. When they pulled up to the rustic lodging, she felt a small sense of relief.

"I promise you that no one will find you here, Sadie," Jay said.

Loud barks rang out as soon as she opened her car door. "Is that a dog?"

"Yes, that's your guard dog. Her name is Zoe. She'll protect you."

"No, I'll protect her," Kip said. His tone firm.

And for the first time since he found out the truth, Kip took her hand and squeezed. She wanted to start crying at his demonstration of loyalty to her. But she needed to be strong right now.

"Whose dog is it?" she asked.

"She's the dog of the local K-9 unit's trainer. She's the best there is, and she's used to working with a lot of different handlers."

"So the local police know about me?"

"No. I just told them that I was bringing a female who was in need of a protection dog. They didn't ask any questions. I've worked with this trainer before on a case years ago. He knows not to push. He's here now.

This is one of his cabins he owns and manages. He rents it out, but it's empty right now."

"Are you sure it's secure here?" Kip asked.

"There's no way anyone will know that the two of you are here." He eyed Sadie. "Especially if she keeps on that heinous wig."

She shuddered. "We'll have to talk about that. Also, if I'm going to be here for a while, I'm going to need you to get my cats and bring them here. I'm not sure if they'll get along with the dog, but we'll figure something out."

"I know how much you love your cats. Don't worry. Once I get a better read on the security situation, then we can get you set up like home. I can't make any promises about going back to El Paso, though."

"And what about Kip?" she asked.

"We'll figure something out. Obviously he wasn't part of the plan."

"Don't worry about me. Sadie's safety is the top priority."

It felt great to stretch her legs as she stepped out of the car. A huge German shepherd ran up to her. A man's voice rang out, and the dog stopped in its tracks. The man walked out of the cabin. He was tall and dressed in a police uniform. She guessed he was in his fifties.

"Zoe, sit," he ordered. The dog sat right in front of Sadie.

"Zoe, guard," he said.

Sadie leaned down, and the dog licked her hands. She surely missed her cats. But there was a sweet look in Zoe's dark brown eyes that put her at ease. This dog would protect her. She knew it. Between Kip and Zoe, she was in good hands.

The man walked over. “Come on in. My name is Barry. And you’ve already met Zoe. She’ll keep you company and stop anyone from messing with you. I guarantee you that.”

Barry shook hands with Jay. “Good to see you again, Jay.”

“It’s beautiful up here,” she said.

“I know. We love it. It’s nice now in the summer. Might be a bit cold for you in the winter, but we don’t have to talk about that right now.”

She didn’t plan to be here in the winter. That was for sure.

“Barry, why don’t you take Sadie and Kip inside?”

They followed Barry who gave her a smile. He seemed like a nice man. Zoe trotted along right beside her with her tail wagging quickly back and forth.

“This cabin’s plenty big. It’s got three bedrooms and two baths. Sadie, you can have the master bedroom. It has its own private bath. So you’ll have all the privacy you need. Kip, I just found out about your arrival, but no issues there. Just take either of the other bedrooms you’d like. Sadie, I just ask that you let Zoe stay in the room with you. It’s best if she’s with you at all times.”

She turned to Barry. “You have no idea what you’ve gotten yourself into with me, do you?”

He laughed. “I can only imagine. But it’s not my job to pry. I know Jay’s a good man. He does the right thing. So anytime I can help him, that’s what I do.”

“Thank you.”

Barry spent some time teaching her the key commands for Zoe—including Guard, Friend and Attack, while Kip conducted a full sweep of the cabin. Zoe seemed excited to have a new friend. Sadie felt calmer just knowing Zoe was there.

She walked through the cabin and was amazed at how large it seemed. As she entered the master bedroom and saw the colorful patchwork quilt covering the bed, it reminded her of how tired she really was. She shut the door for a moment of much-needed privacy.

Zoe's cold nose nudged her hand. Sadie knelt down to rub her furry ears. "We're going to get through this, Zoe." Zoe's tail wagged even quicker, and she was impressed with how the dog picked up on her cues. Seeing Zoe made her realize how much she wanted to meet Kip's dog, Colby. She quickly pushed that thought out of her mind. There could be no future now with Kip. It's something she'd just have to accept. Even if he would eventually forgive her, he would never trust her again. Zoe nuzzled up to her, and she let the tears flow freely. It was just her and Zoe. And she didn't have to be tough. Right now she could let it out—all the pain and frustration. And loss.

After a few minutes there was a light knock at the door. "You okay in there?" Kip asked.

She wiped the tears from her eyes and pulled herself together. "You can come in," she said quietly.

Kip walked through the door. "Are you sure you're all right? You've been through a lot. If you need some time I understand that."

"I'll be fine. Like I always am."

Zoe danced around by her feet.

"I see you made quick friends with her."

"She has taken a liking to me. I think I do better with animals than people. I usually don't attract people but repel them."

"Don't say that." He reached out and touched her arm. As he did, Zoe turned all her attention to him and growled. "Whoa, there, Zoe."

"It's okay, Zoe. He's a friend. I guess it's good to know that she can do her job."

Only then did Zoe step back away from Kip.

"Barry left. I told him we would be fine."

"What are you going to do?" she asked.

"Keep you safe. Just like I said. Jay said he has another agent who will be working with us. Between all of us, you'll have round-the-clock protection."

"In addition to your cute guard dog," Jay said as he walked into the room.

She turned her attention to Jay. "Are we sure we can trust another agent? What if he's been bought off by Igor?"

"I can guarantee you that it isn't true. And it's not a he, it's a she."

"Oh." She actually hadn't ever dealt with any females in Witness Protection. The former marshals she'd dealt with had all been men. The women who were around her at the very beginning were all social workers aiding Witness Protection but not actual agents.

"Don't tell me you're sexist. Look at you. You're a top-notch P.I."

"Of course I'm not sexist. I just haven't met any female marshals in the program."

"You'll like her. And she's the only person in this world I knew I could trust."

"How do you know that?"

He looked directly into her eyes and took a step forward. "Because she's my sister."

"Wow. How crazy is that? Is she older or younger?"

"Younger. But only by a year. We're super close. And I know she'd never turn on me. She should be here any minute. We usually don't work together, but I made an exception. Things will get better, Sadie. I promise."

She looked up at him. "Don't make promises you can't keep, Jay. You know I'm still searching for answers. I can't rest until I have them. And now I'm concerned I never will. What could my father have been caught up in? You promise me that you don't know?"

"I've told you before, I was never told. Once I got your case five years ago, that was never an issue."

"Can you find out? Surely someone in the FBI knows."

"Sadie, you know this isn't the time to be poking around," Kip said. "I promise I'll do what I can to look into it once the threat is neutralized."

"It's exactly the time," she said.

Zoe started barking and running around. Although the discussion was interrupted, Sadie couldn't keep her gaze off Kip. She wished she knew what he was thinking.

Jay stepped to the door. "That's got to be my sis. Her name is Val."

She wasn't going to let this topic go. He might be saved by his sister now, but she definitely wouldn't forget.

Sadie and Kip walked downstairs. She saw Jay embracing his sister.

Val pulled back from the hug. She could've been Jay's twin. Tall, dark and thin, she was the female version of Jay.

"You must be Sadie," Val said with an outreached hand and a smile.

"That's me."

"And I'm Val. You're a tough lady to put up with my overbearing brother." She punched Jay in the arm. It was evident that they had a strong relationship.

Zoe circled around Val's legs.

"It's okay, Zoe. She's a friend." Sadie reached over and touched Val's arm, and Zoe's tail started thumping again.

"And this is Kip," Sadie said.

Kip took Val's hand. "I'll let you two ladies get acquainted and have some time together. I'm going to take a shower."

Jay stepped forward. "And I'm going to run into town and stock up on some additional supplies. That okay with you two?"

Val rolled her big brown eyes. "Go. We'll be fine. And we'll gossip about you while you're gone." She winked at Sadie.

Jay grumbled something and then laughed.

Val grabbed her hand. "Let's sit and have a chat."

"I'll be right upstairs if you two need anything," Kip said.

Val took off her suit jacket, and Sadie couldn't help but notice the gun holstered to her side.

Sadie sat on the couch, and Zoe lounged by her feet. Val sat beside her on the sofa.

"Where do we even begin?" Val asked.

"How much has Jay told you?"

"Nothing beyond the fact that he needed my help immediately. We didn't want to talk on our cells."

"Well," she said as she reached down and patted Zoe's head. "It's a long story."

"We've got all night. I'm not going anywhere."

And it took over an hour for Sadie to rehash the entire story, top to bottom, not leaving out any details. Kip had given them their privacy, popping in once to make sure they were okay. He surely didn't want to be in the middle of their conversation. He was probably plotting something. As she was winding down, she looked over at Val. "What's taking Jay so long?"

"I don't know." Val frowned. "Let me call him." She picked up her phone and dialed. She waited. "It went to voice mail."

Sadie made eye contact with Val, and they were both thinking the same thing. Something was wrong. "It could be that he's just out of cell range up here in the mountains," Sadie suggested.

"That's possible. But I don't want to take any unnecessary risks. I'd like to do a security sweep of the cabin. Stay here."

When Val didn't return after a few minutes, Sadie grew concerned.

"Kip," Sadie called out. Then Zoe's ears perked up.

Kip ran down the stairs taking them two at a time. "What's wrong?"

"We couldn't get in contact with Jay. Then Val wanted to do a security sweep, but she hasn't come back yet."

He reached over and pulled her to him. "We may need to get out of here."

Glass broke behind her—a shot whizzed by her ear. She hit the ground and planned to stay low.

"Stay down, Sadie," he said.

They could try to exit through the back. But what if someone was out there waiting for her?

Kip slid down beside her. "I'll cover you. Make a run for the back door."

"And if someone's there?"

"Shoot to kill," Kip said.

Sadie nodded. Kip put his hand on Sadie's. "Sadie, this isn't the time to shy away from using that gun. You're highly trained. It's either our lives or his. This is justified."

"I don't know what happened to Val."

"It's okay. I'll handle everything here. Then I'll come and get you. Find someplace secure to hide with Zoe."

Panic ripped through her body. This was it. They were trapped. And she had no clue where Val was.

Sadie looked at Zoe. She had no idea if Zoe would follow or stay behind. Would she even listen to her? Once Barry had given the guard command, he was probably the only one who could break it. She hated to put Zoe in danger. But she hoped that the attacker would target her and not the dog.

"On three," Kip said. "One, two, three."

Sadie sprinted for the back door with Zoe in tow. A few shots rang out, but she didn't turn back. She prayed as she ran through the back door and outside into the backyard. She kept running into the dark woods. She had no idea where she was going or if anyone was following her. Zoe seemed comfortable. Maybe she knew the woods. "You lead, Zoe. I'll follow."

As if Zoe understood, she took charge, and Sadie ran behind her through the woods. Ducking and moving around all the huge tree limbs and debris. Thank the Lord it wasn't winter. But it was still cool in the mountains at night. Would she be able to survive out here? Could she find help before Igor or his men found her?

While all of those thoughts rang through her head, she kept pace with Zoe. And prayed that Kip and Val were okay. She feared the worse for Jay.

Sadie didn't know how far she and Zoe had run. Her body ached, and she struggled to catch her breath as the cool breeze filled the air. Knowing she couldn't go much longer, she whispered to Zoe. "Zoe, stay."

The dog stopped in her tracks. Sadie sat down against a large tree and held Zoe close to her. "Do you hear anything, girl?"

Zoe didn't seem particularly on alert. Maybe they'd put some distance between them and whoever was coming after her.

"What are we going to do?" A chill ran through her as she assessed the situation. She needed to keep moving, and the only help she had was Zoe. Thank God for her. But with no supplies, neither of them would make it very long in the Rockies. If Kip made it, he would come looking for her. She was sure of it. But what if he hadn't? That thought made her sick. Igor's killing had to stop.

She had to find her way back to civilization and then figure out what to do. It was so dark; the moon provided the only light. She needed some serious guidance from God right about now. Which way to go? There were so many options. Zoe nudged her hand, and she prayed that Zoe would be able to lead her to safety. *Please, Lord—protect us both right now.* She also said another prayer for everyone's safety.

Sadie continued to let Zoe lead. Still a long night ahead—assuming they both survived. Sadie felt as if she and Zoe had been hiking through the woods for hours. Her feet were killing her, and she was pushing forward only on adrenaline. When she stopped to lean up against a tree for a brief moment of respite, that's when she heard the crunching noise. Someone was closing in on her, and she had missed the sounds until now.

Zoe started barking loudly, and Sadie feared the noise would give away her location. She started running, knowing that was her only hope. She could hear the loud footsteps bearing down behind her. This was it. She was going to die. She couldn't take the risk of stopping to try to get off a shot—her only hope was to outrun him.

She felt like she had put some distance between her and the assailant. She couldn't even hear the footsteps. But now was no time to rest. She'd lost Zoe somewhere along the way. Had Zoe slowed him down?

As she ran by a large tree, a big mass jumped out in front of her. It was too late. She ran directly into him. Right into the arms of the man she feared the most. Igor Vladimir.

ELEVEN

Kip searched the cabin. The shooter was long gone. He'd found Val knocked out on the front porch. There was still no word from Jay. And of course, Sadie was out there somewhere alone and being hunted by Igor and his men. He had to find her.

He called in the police and FBI. He wasn't going to wait for them to get there. He had to start searching those woods. But there was also one more call he needed to make before he headed out on his search. He pulled out his cell phone and dialed the number that he had tried to erase from his memory. Brad answered on the third ring.

"Kip? Is that you?" he asked.

"Yeah, it's me," he said, his voice low.

"What's wrong, man? Can't say I ever expected to hear from you again. You know. After everything."

"I've got a situation. Are you in town?"

"I'm actually out in Colorado at my cabin. You remember that place, right? We went there once before our first deployment?"

"Yes." He thanked the Lord and breathed a sigh of relief. "I do."

Kip proceeded to provide as much detail as he could over the phone. Brad took it all in and asked a lot of questions.

"Here's the address," he told him. "Can you meet me here as soon as you can?"

"Kip, this isn't the right time for me to issue apologies. So I'll just say that I'm here for whatever you need. I'll be over as soon as I can."

"Thank you." He'd never expected to have to talk to Brad again. But Sadie's life was on the line, and he would do anything for her. Even if she hadn't been honest about her true self. She was actually doing the right thing. She had followed protocol. It was hard to fault her for that. He understood the importance of witness safety. Even if it hurt him that she couldn't have told him about her past. He'd fallen for her, and he certainly wasn't ready to let her go.

Kip felt warm, almost as if he was running a fever. It had to be the stress. He'd been through some unimaginable things in his life as an army ranger. But the absolute fear and dread he was feeling right now for Sadie was even worse. He felt helpless. That summed it up.

He'd searched the woods for hours all night long and found nothing. Finally, he went back to the cabin to meet with the authorities.

He had turned away from his faith for too long. He needed the Lord to get through this. He understood that. He also knew that Sadie had amazingly strong faith. She would fight, and God would protect her. He couldn't believe that this would be the end for her. She was still young and had so much life left to lead. So much to give. Even in the short time he'd known her, she'd changed his life forever. Filling his heart with faith and love again. Faith in God, a love for her and a respect for himself again.

Sadie's arms felt heavy, and her neck ached. Where was she? Light streamed in from a window, but it hurt to open her eyes. Her vision blurred. Then she took in a deep breath. The realization hit her. Igor. He'd taken her.

She was sitting in a hard wooden chair, with her hands handcuffed behind her. No doubt he'd taken her gun. Where was he? She took a moment to try to assess her surroundings. Another cabin. This one not nearly as nice as Barry's. She was in the living room. The only other furniture was a beat-up sofa and a ragged chair. She could see the dark musty kitchen from where she was sitting.

She knew as surely as she was still breathing that she wouldn't be alive for long if Igor had his way. The fact that he didn't kill her immediately scared her even more. What did he have in mind? Torture? She tried to put those thoughts aside and develop a strategy. Was there anything she could do to save herself? She was great at talking herself out of situations, but she'd gotten in so deep on this one. Igor would be out for revenge—just as she had been. The embarrassment of being duped by a woman wouldn't help either. Their past couldn't be undone.

She still had nightmares about the day Igor had killed her parents. She could hear the *pop*, *pop*, *pop* of gunshots. She had been so young. Hearing the noises that sounded like firecrackers had made her afraid. She'd walked down the stairs and saw an unspeakable horror. Igor standing over her parents' lifeless bodies. Her entire life. Shattered. Taken away all too soon. Because Igor, little more than a child himself at eighteen, had walked into her house and shot her mom and dad in cold blood. Why?

Even if Igor was going to kill her, she needed answers. Why? Why? Why? What could've been so important that he'd broken into her house and shot them both? And she'd never forget the look in his eyes as he saw her standing there on the stairs trembling as she gripped her teddy bear. For a moment, she thought he might raise his gun at her. But for some reason he didn't. He'd looked at her with disdain. Maybe even pity. Then he'd run out the door.

She was left with a broken life. Social services had taken her in. But it wasn't long before Witness Protection took over. And when she was being ripped apart by that defense attorney on the stand, she'd known she'd never be the same. How badly she wished she could've done more to make Igor pay for his crimes. A tear slid down her cheek. Look where her pursuit of revenge had gotten her. Deep down she knew that she should've never have gone after Igor. She was safe. Had a good life and job. But no matter what she did, she could never forget him. Never forget how he had wronged her. And while she prayed every day that God would help her move past her anger and quest for revenge, it was her greatest failing. Because she hadn't moved on. And now, because of that, she would most likely be killed by the same man who killed her parents.

A door slammed, and she jumped. Igor strode through the front door, his eyes blazing with anger.

"Ms. Lane, you leave me speechless." He paused.

"Or actually, I guess I need to be calling you Ms. Mars. Lydia Mars."

She couldn't let him see weakness. No fear. Not now. "Lydia died years ago. You're responsible for her death." She refused to break eye contact. She had to find out what was driving this man.

"You are so wrong, Lydia. I saved you."

"By killing my parents. By forcing me into Witness Protection. By taking away everything I loved. Destroying the life of an eight-year-old girl?"

"You have no idea."

"I wish I did. I'm here now. Why don't you give me the answers?"

He paced back and forth clenching his fists as he walked. Then he turned to her. "You really have no clue, do you?"

"Why you murdered my family in cold blood? No, I have no idea. No one has ever been able to tell me."

"Your mother," he said with narrowed eyes. "You do not know the truth about your mother." She had no idea what he was talking about. Was he delusional?

Then he turned away for a minute. She sat afraid of what his next move might be. When he twisted around to face her, his face reddened. A vein popped up on the top of his forehead. Was this going to be it? He looked like he could kill her with his bare hands.

"Tell me what you know," she said evenly.

"Your mother was an undercover FBI agent."

"What?" There was no way. Her mom was a librarian. Right? Sadie had only been eight years old when she died, but she remembered her mom's occupation vividly. She'd loved to read and often read books to Sadie at night.

"But that's not the reason why I killed her."

She sucked in a breath. Her heart pounded.

"Your mother seduced my father. She had evidence against him. She gave him an ultimatum. Either he would turn himself in or she would do it."

"This is crazy."

"It's the truth," he yelled. "My father is such a weak man. He fell for your mother's clever ruse. I was smarter than him, even as a boy. I saw her come and go. I knew something was wrong. Terribly wrong. I never trusted her. They broke it off. But years later, she was back in his life. In our lives. Then one day I overhear her threatening him. Everything. Everything we worked for. Everything our family built. Would be gone. Because of one woman. I had no choice."

"You always have a choice, Igor. You were just eighteen. Why didn't you let your father fight his own battles?"

"Because he wouldn't! He loved your mother. For some reason I will never understand. Even after he found out that she had used him. Set him up. He still loved her."

"Why kill my father?"

"I wasn't trying to. He took the first bullet aimed for your mother. Crazy man. Sacrificing his life for hers."

She couldn't believe all of this. It was so much to comprehend. Her entire understanding of her childhood—of her birth parents—had just been flipped upside down. She had to ask the final question though. The one that haunted her each day.

"Then why didn't you kill me?"

"Because of what your mother told me seconds before I killed her."

"And what is that?"

He looked down and then back up again taking a few steps closer. Then he knelt down in front of her. "You're my half sister."

Sadie felt her mouth drop open. This couldn't be true. There was no way. Her mother would've never actually cheated on her father. And had a child with another man? Impossible! But the timing. She thought back to the date of her parents' marriage. Could her mother have been with Sergei before her parents got married? Oh no. "No. No. There's no way."

"Believe me I was skeptical too. I thought she was just trying to save her young child's life. What you would expect out of a mother who knew she was about to die. I was also very young. In that moment, I couldn't make that decision. Looking at you and not knowing. I had a moment of sentimental weakness. So I left you there. And then you testified against me."

"Look at us. We don't look alike. It's not possible."

"Unfortunately, it is. And even though you don't look like me, I certainly see the resemblance between you Artur. Now that I know, it is quite striking. I had a DNA test run from a hairbrush my men collected when your true identity came to my attention earlier this week. They said your house in El Paso is quite charming. However, the DNA test is undeniable proof." He paused. "I'm certain you are my half sister."

She was speechless. She was a part of the Vladimir family. The family that had killed her parents.

He leaned down until he was inches away from her face. "You are just like your traitor of a mother. I should've killed you eighteen years ago." He spit in her face, and she recoiled.

"But because you've made such a mess of my life yet again, I'm going to make you pay. I know you care about that FBI suit Kip. He'll come looking for you. I'm sure of it." He paused taking a step back, "And when he does, you'll watch him die."

Pain ripped through her body as he slapped her hard across the face. But she wouldn't let him see her cry. She'd die first. She started praying again. When his fist connected to her face again, her world turned to darkness.

Kip walked through Barry's cabin which was full of FBI agents and a local police presence. The thought of sleeping never crossed his mind. It was barely dawn, and he was ready to put in a plan of action because his first search had failed. He wasn't going to fail again. He'd also been working all his FBI contacts and briefed the agents on the scene. He was going to update the DEA contact named Agent Maynard that he'd tracked down thanks to one of the FBI agent's laptops. Maynard was en route to Colorado. It was time to bust this thing wide open. They needed every resource available tracking Igor so they could find Sadie. Hopefully, the DEA would have some additional insights or resources.

"Agent Maynard, it's Agent Moore."

"We just landed in Denver," Agent Maynard said.

"We?"

"Yeah. I've got company with me. Related to our suspect."

Kip couldn't believe it. Had Agent Maynard brought Artur with him? "Why did you bring him?"

"He says he wants to help. He also has some information you're going to want to hear. I can't discuss it over this line."

"Understood. We're using a cabin of one of the local police officers as our operating base. I'll text you the address."

Loud barking caught Kip's attention. He hung up on Agent Maynard and saw Zoe pawing at the back door.

Barry ran toward the door. "Zoe," he yelled as he opened the door. The dog limped into the room and nuzzled Barry's hand before lying down at his feet. Barry looked close to tears. Had Zoe left Sadie, or had they been forced apart? Kip got a sick feeling in his stomach and prayed for Sadie's safety. Barry had said that once he gave the guard command that Zoe would never leave Sadie voluntarily. He believed in his dog, and Kip really had no reason to doubt him.

"How's she look?" Kip asked, crouching down near Zoe.

"A little banged up. But seems she will be walking just fine after a little rest. I think she's just dehydrated and has muscle fatigue. I'll clean her up and check for any other injuries."

"I'll help." Kip needed something to take his mind off the endless waiting. Everyone was in plan-of-attack mode. Not attack mode. Kip just wanted to get out there again and keep looking for Sadie. But the clues were limited at best. And the woods were beyond expansive. No one really knew what Igor's endgame was. Except that it was most likely deadly.

After he'd assisted in cleaning up Zoe and helping check her out, he felt pretty sure that she would be fine.

Brad walked over to him. "Can we talk?" he asked in a low tone.

Kip nodded. They walked into one of the guest rooms.

"I've got a lot to say to you. I know this isn't the time. But given the circumstances maybe it is." Brad closed his eyes for a second and then opened them back up making direct eye contact.

"I love Lacy. I'm not going to apologize for that. And I love my baby. But what I did to you was wrong. Absolutely one-hundred percent. I take the blame. It wasn't her fault. It was all mine."

Kip shook his head. "It takes two," Kip said softly.

"But I was the man. I was the one to pursue. You should know that I've changed a lot about my life. I've found Christ. I started going to church, and I asked God to forgive me. I know you'll probably never forgive me. But I do ask for your forgiveness. You're a better man than I'll ever be."

As he looked into Brad's dark eyes and saw the pain, he was moved. Because his own pain and concern for Sadie was so great. "I'll do my best. Thanks for coming out here to help."

"It was the least I could do." He paused. "But there's one more thing that I have to get off my chest. It's been eating at me. No matter how much I pray—I can't shake it. The guilt is bad, Kip. It's never ending." He hung his head low. "You were right. About the village operation in Iraq. We should've done something to stop that massacre. I made the wrong call. I was weak. And afraid. I've never thought of myself as a weak man. I've always prided myself on being tough and macho. But that tour in Iraq, when I had to see the devastation and know that we could've at least done something to make it better—if we'd all committed to it and gone in—I don't know that I will ever get over it. But I wanted to make sure that you knew that I take the responsibility for that. You fought for us to go in. So much so that you made some enemies on the team. You were in the right. And if I could do everything over, I would've listened to you."

Kip's heart broke listening to Brad's normally strong voice shaking. Tears welled up in Brad's eyes. Kip wanted to harbor anger and resentment. But at that moment he simply couldn't. This man was hurting just like he was. Yeah, he'd done wrong by him with Lacy. No doubt. The look on Brad's face while talking about the operation in Iraq hit him hard. Brad hadn't forgotten and moved on. Just like him, Brad was carrying around a boatload of guilt. And most importantly, Brad had found Christ.

"Brad, we all have to carry the burden of what happened there. It's not just on you," Kip said.

"But it should be," he whispered.

"No. We went in there as a team. We left as a team. And we shoulder responsibility as a team."

"I appreciate you saying that."

"I mean it. And you're right. It's been hard to forgive you. Almost impossible, but I'm trying. You see, I've moved on. I love another woman now. And that's what I want to focus on. I just want to find Sadie."

"We'll do everything we can." Brad gave Kip a bear hug and patted him on the back.

They heard Zoe barking. "That must be Agent Maynard and Artur. This should be interesting."

* * *

Sadie woke up, and her mouth was dry. Her head was throbbing, and her left eye was swollen shut. She almost wished she'd stayed unconscious longer. The pain was horrendous. Cautiously, she looked around and didn't see Igor. He was probably out there somewhere planning his next move. He wanted Kip to pay with his life. This was all her fault. She'd put Kip in grave danger.

She closed her eyes and wondered how this had all happened. It was bad enough that she already had a second identity. To now hear that she was also someone else entirely shook her to the core. And her mother! An FBI agent having a relationship with Sergei Vladimir. Had her mother loved Sergei? Had her mother loved the man Sadie had thought was her biological father?

She sighed knowing that she'd probably never know the full truth of what happened. She racked her brain to remember details about her mother. She had fond memories of her. Thinking back to her mom reading to her at the library. Though she wasn't a librarian, but an FBI agent. At least according to Igor. Why would he make up a story like that? She couldn't help but feel a moment of anger toward her mother. Her job had gotten both her parents killed. And she could've been killed too.

Everything made sense now, though. Why the FBI was so involved in her case. The FBI agent she blamed all these years was probably perfectly innocent. It was her mother who had put her entire family in danger. She'd made so many faulty assumptions about the FBI, about her father—and obviously now about her mother. She'd painted her mother as an innocent bystander for the last twenty years. Knowing the truth was difficult but also liberating. She'd wanted answers, and now she had them.

She also had to face the very real possibility that Igor could succeed in his murderous plot. She prayed that God would keep her and Kip safe. If it was her time, she would be okay with that. But she couldn't let Kip pay the price for her desire for revenge.

Igor—her half brother. The implication of that was mind-boggling. Sergei Vladimir was her biological father. She took in a breath just thinking about it. Did her adoptive parents know? The FBI probably kept it from them, too.

She felt incredibly woozy. The sharp cutting pain in her head was too much. She had to close her eyes. Even though she knew she probably shouldn't if she had a concussion. But the pain took over.

Kip eyed Agent Maynard and Artur with skepticism. Now standing under the cabin lights, he got his first good look at the pair. Agent Maynard was tall with shaggy dark hair and a full beard. He didn't look like a typical suit. The DEA types often went undercover, and his look was consistent with that. Kip was struck again by how different Artur looked from his brother Igor.

After everyone made introductions, the men gathered around the dining room table, pulling up extra chairs. Barry passed around the coffeepot, and everyone filled up their cups. It was going to be a long day ahead. Zoe had taken a real liking to him, and she'd curled up right by his feet. The poor dog was exhausted after her trauma in the woods.

"Before we jump into our search efforts, Artur has something to explain. We should all be aware of these additional facts because I'm sure they impact Igor's strategy and plans."

Kip's gut clenched in worry. What could Artur know? He felt as if he wasn't going to like it. He braced himself for the worst.

"There's no easy way to explain this," Artur said. "So, I'll just say it. Sadie is my half sister."

"What?" Kip heard himself ask loudly.

Artur nodded. "It is true. Sadie's mother worked for the FBI. But she developed a personal relationship with my father. That's when she became pregnant with Sadie. But instead of staying with my father, she ended up leaving him and marrying Sadie's father. Years later, though, after she gained more experience with the FBI, Sadie's mother gave our father an ultimatum—turn himself in to the FBI or she would do it. Igor found out about this. He saw Sadie's mother as a traitor—not just to our father but to our whole family. So he killed both Sadie's mother and her father that night. That's when Igor found out from Sadie's mom that eight-year-old Sadie was actually Sergei's child. Igor spared her life. But after everything that has happened, I am certain he will try to kill her now."

Kip couldn't stay seated. He stood up and started pacing back and forth behind the dining room table, furiously trying to make sense of everything he was hearing. Zoe started whining down by his legs. He kneeled, soothing Zoe by saying, "It's okay, girl." But the words he said were a lie. He didn't believe them one bit. Zoe cocked her head to the side as if she were able to read his mind.

"Everyone needs to stay calm," Agent Maynard said. "This is valuable information. And Igor probably doesn't realize that we know this. We can use that to our advantage. Based on this set of facts, I agree that Sadie is in grave danger."

Kip returned to the table and took a seat. "What are we going to do about it? We are running out of time. He may have already killed her." His voice was strained. He was thinking with his heart right now, not his head.

Brad stood up. "We should expand our quadrant search. Break into teams and search this mountain piece by piece."

"And what if he's taken her somewhere else?"

"Then we'll hear about it. Because if his goal was just to kill her, he could do that here on the mountain. If he moves her, that means he's looking for something else."

Kip was grateful that Brad was thinking clearly. "Brad's right. Let's break into teams and start searching. We need to use every ounce of daylight we have. Any updates on Val from the hospital?"

"She's in surgery. It's touch and go," Barry said. "He really did a number on her. And no one has been able to make contact with Jay. We can only assume that Igor or his men got to him."

The men broke into two-man teams—except that Kip insisted on Zoe going with him as his partner. Zoe was used to working with different handlers because she was often used as a training dog. They were well stocked on high-tech equipment; Kip had his top-of-the-line GPS with him. But he felt that Zoe might be his best asset. She might be able to track Sadie's scent.

"Everyone has their cell phone. Let's stay in touch. Check in every hour, on the hour, with home base. Barry will stay here at the cabin with Artur in case there are any developments," Agent Maynard said. "Understand?"

Everyone knew what they had to do. Kip was ready. He had his search grid, but he would deviate if Zoe gave him any indication that she was on to something. He checked his watch. Seven a.m. A full day ahead as the sun peaked through the clouds. If they didn't find her today, he was worried they never would. At least not alive. He didn't know where that feeling was coming from, but he couldn't deny it. He prayed that she was hunkered down somewhere. Safe. And waiting for rescue. He knew that wasn't the most likely option.

Pulling on his backpack of supplies, he was ready to move. He had plenty of water for him and Zoe, plus food for them both. "Okay, Zoe. Find Sadie," he said. *Dear Lord, I know I've turned away from You for far too long. Sadie helped show me the way back to You. Now I need You to help me find my way to her. Please keep her safe from harm.*

Zoe took off, and he was right behind. He gave her enough room to work, but kept her in his sights. After a couple of hours, his frustration was mounting. He felt like Zoe was starting to wander in circles. He was about to take over and have her follow him, when Zoe stopped. She just sat there sniffing into the air. Given her top physical condition, he didn't think she was too tired.

"What is it, girl?"

Then she sprinted away—as if she was on a mission of her very own. There was no way she was getting away from him. He ran as fast as he could to close the gap. Then he saw what Zoe was running toward. A small cabin!

Could Sadie be in there? Was this what he'd been praying for? Knowing he couldn't get emotional, he called Zoe back with as light of a voice as he could. They couldn't just run in there and bust the door down—as much as he wanted to. This may be their only shot. He pulled out his phone and started to text the coordinates to the team.

"I'd put that down if you ever want to see Sadie alive again, Agent Moore."

Igor. He'd know that voice anywhere. Slowly, he turned and saw the monster staring at him with a wide, sinister grin and a gun pointed at his chest.

"I knew you'd come for her," he said while looking at Zoe, then turned his attention back to Kip. "I thought it was a nice touch sending the dog back. She led you to me. I thought you'd stick close to the dog because you knew that would be your best hope of tracking Sadie."

"Igor, it's over. We've got an entire team of federal agents swarming this mountain. Turn yourself in now. Before it's too late."

Igor laughed loudly.

"How did you find Sadie here?"

"You're in no position to be asking questions. It's irrelevant to your current predicament. Although Sadie's agent did refuse to give up her location. I was impressed by that. The fool made the mistake of bringing his sister here—thinking she could protect Sadie if he couldn't. That didn't turn out too well for them did it? How is she doing by the way? Did she end up like her brother? He had a pretty nasty gunshot wound. Will either of them even survive?"

"You really are pure evil." Igor disgusted him. How

could he rationalize with a person who had no conscience and absolutely no moral compass?

"I take that as a compliment." Igor paused and bobbed his gun up and down. "I said, drop the phone."

He knew he had no choice. Out of the corner of his eye, he saw Zoe backing away. *Dear God, please don't let him hurt the innocent dog.* Zoe looked over at Kip, and he nodded. Saying another prayer. "Go, Zoe, Go!" Zoe sprinted away from them back into the woods. Igor had to make the choice. Take his gun off of Kip to shoot at Zoe, or keep his gun on Kip. Kip knew exactly what he would have to do. Igor couldn't risk Kip getting to his weapon.

Igor cursed. "They will never find us in time. So it won't matter if she leads anyone back here. Now slowly remove your gun and place it on the ground."

Kip needed to buy every second he could. While Igor might not think Zoe could lead help back in time, he had faith in her. Especially if she ran into any of the other teams on the way.

"What's your real goal here, Igor?"

"Enough stalling. Put the gun down. Now."

Kip didn't want to push Igor too hard, but he felt he had some leverage. Igor obviously didn't want to kill him this second. He could've done that by now. He feared that Igor had a plan involving both him and Sadie. He had to stop him before he could hurt her.

"Where's Sadie?"

"Are you trying to get shot?" Igor asked.

"Not particularly. I've been shot before. It's not the greatest feeling."

Igor's nose flared in anger. "Now!" he yelled.

Kip slowly reached for his gun. He pulled it from

his holster and then knelt down to the ground placing it there.

"Let's move inside."

Igor pointed the gun at him, and Kip started walking. He was afraid of what he was going to see behind that door.

They walked up the steps, and Igor pushed the gun into his back. "Open the door slowly," he instructed.

He did as he was told and took a cautious step through the front door. Then his heart dropped. In the tiny living room sat Sadie. Tied to a chair and handcuffed. She was badly beaten. One of her eyes was black and swollen, and there was blood all over her face. Her eye widened when she saw him, but she didn't speak.

He wanted to kill Igor right then with his bare hands. He would've risked it if it was just his own life. But he couldn't take the chance that Sadie would get shot in the process.

"We have a little reunion of sorts." Igor tipped his head to the side. He pulled another chair from across the room and placed it directly across from Sadie. "See, Sadie's going to watch as I make you pay. Then I'll deal with her long after you're dead."

This was even worse than he'd feared. He had to find a way to stall. Seconds could be lifesaving. *God, please let Zoe lead help here before it's too late.* His heart broke into a million pieces as he looked at Sadie. She was trying to keep it together, but he could tell she was in great distress. He had to do something.

"Igor, don't be so melodramatic."

Igor raised an eyebrow at him.

"You really think Sadie cares about me? She just used me to get to you. I know that now. Why would I care what happens to her?" He prayed that Sadie knew he was just putting on an act.

"And you expect me to believe that? If you didn't care for her then why would you have come after her?"

Kip laughed. "I wasn't coming after her, Igor. I was coming after you." Kip could see the wheels churning in Igor's brain. He'd at least put a shred of doubt into his mind. "You're a wanted man. By multiple government agencies. I plan to bring you in. I'm going to take the credit for this bust. It will be the biggest of my career."

"Enough talk," Igor snapped. "Sit down in that chair."

Kip walked slowly over to the chair and sat down.

"Now. Handcuff yourself behind your back." Igor threw him a pair of cuffs. Igor was being smart not to get too close to Kip. He probably worried that Kip could take him down. And he was right. Kip took the cuffs and reluctantly cuffed himself. Although it would take a lot more than a pair of cuffs to stop him.

"So, sis. How you feeling now?" Igor asked as he walked closer to Sadie. Kip was careful not to show any emotion.

Then Kip heard something. Very faint. There was a noise though. He prayed that he wasn't hearing things. He needed to keep Igor talking.

Sadie looked up at Igor. "I don't have anything to say to you. And you're not my brother."

Igor raised an eyebrow. "You can't run from your destiny, Sadie. Deep down, you're just like me. You're a Vladimir. You're not one of the good guys. It's not in your blood."

Kip heard another creaking noise. Or at least he

thought he did. "What are you two talking about?" Kip asked, playing dumb.

"Ah, you don't know the truth. I forget these things. Sadie here is my sister. Her mother was an undercover FBI agent. Much like yourself. Things didn't end too well for her. And they're not going to end well for you. I think I've had a change of heart. Sadie, you're going to be the one to kill Kip. Not me."

Her eyes widened. This was not good.

Then the back door flew open. Shots rang out in rapid succession. Kip pushed himself up from his chair and jumped onto Sadie trying to guard her body with his own. Her chair fell backward taking him and his chair with them. More shots. He felt something burning in his shoulder. Then there was nothing.

TWELVE

Blood poured on top of Sadie. But she didn't think it was her own. She didn't feel like she'd been shot. Kip! His body and his half-broken chair were on top of her. Zoe stood nudging her face. She had no idea what was going on. The gunfire had been deafening. She'd counted at least five shots. Who else had been hit?

Then a muscular man came over to her and knelt down on the floor. "Sadie?" he asked.

"Yes," she said weakly.

"I'm Brad Sullivan. Have you been shot?" he asked calmly.

"No. The blood is Kip's. Please help him."

Brad lifted Kip's body off of hers as if it didn't weigh anything. "We need a medic now. I'll try to stop the bleeding."

"Brad?" she asked softly.

"Yes."

"You're *the* Brad?"

"Yes, ma'am. I'm guessing you haven't heard many very nice things about me. And I'm sad to say everything Kip told you was true."

She watched as Brad tore off part of Kip's shirt and applied pressure to Kip's shoulder.

Zoe nudged her cold nose against her face.

"What happened to Igor?"

"I shot him. He didn't make it."

She let out a sigh of relief as the tears flowed freely. And then she prayed that Kip would pull through this. Now was no time to focus on revenge. Igor was dead. It was over. Finally.

Another man squatted down beside her. Then she opened her good eye wider. She recognized him. "Artur?" she asked.

"Hello, sister. I am so sorry." He gently touched her cheek. "Hey, guys, let's get her out of this chair."

A couple of other men she didn't recognize worked on her. First removing the handcuffs and then lifting her out of the chair carefully.

"What hurts?" one of them asked.

"Everything." She paused. "I think I have a slight concussion. I've been fading in and out."

Artur shook his head. "I am so sorry I didn't stop him sooner. So, so sorry." She saw the tears well up in Artur's dark eyes. Eyes that she now saw matched her own. She was overcome with emotion as so many feelings gripped her heart.

"Kip," she said. Kip had to make to it.

"The medics are here. They're transporting him to the hospital. You will be next," Artur said.

She closed her eyes.

Kip woke up feeling like he'd been shot. Wait, he *had* been shot. His eyes popped open, and he instantly knew he was in a hospital. The buzzing of the equipment, the lighting and the smell told him so.

Sadie! Where was she? Was she alive?

"You're awake," a tender voice said.

He looked over and there she was. Was he dreaming? "Sadie?" he asked.

"Yes, it's me." She grabbed his hand.

"You're okay?" He eyed the bandage across her eyebrow.

"Yes. I'm fine. Thanks to you. And you'll be good as new soon, too. Thanks to Brad."

"Brad? What happened?"

"Brad shot Igor. And you threw yourself on top of me blocking Igor's shot. I'm so sorry I got you into all this. It's my fault that you got shot. But it could've been so much worse. Thank God Brad was able to get there in time. And thank God for Zoe. That dog is truly a blessing."

"Is Brad okay? What about Jay and Zoe?"

"Yes. Brad is perfectly fine. And Zoe is too." She paused and a single tear rolled down her cheek. "They found Jay. Igor shot him. They rushed him to the hospital. It's touch and go."

"And Igor?"

"Igor didn't make it. He died from Brad's first shot. He said he couldn't take the risk in going for a disabling shot. He made the right call."

"Sadie, all that stuff I said. I promise, I didn't mean any of it. I was just trying to stall and throw Igor off."

"I realized that. At first I was shocked, and then there was something about the way you said it and looked at me. I got the message."

"I'm so glad."

"Of course, I have a lot of explaining to do. But not right now. You're under strict orders to rest. In addition to the gunshot wound, you've got cracked ribs. I'm not supposed to keep you up but for a few minutes at a time."

He closed his eyes. "I'm fine. I really am. Keep talking." And he drifted away.

Sadie stayed by Kip's bedside around the clock. After everything that had happened, she refused to leave him. She'd even brought Sammie and Leo over to his house, and they were getting along better with Colby than she could have ever imagined. Colby let the cats believe they were in charge. And he loved having extra friends around.

It had been a week and she was exhausted but so thankful that Kip was going to make a full recovery. Even though Jay had lost a ton of blood from the gunshot wound, he was going to make it. Jay would be away from work for a while, doing some serious rehab on his shoulder. It was truly a blessing that he survived. In the end, technology had been their undoing, since Igor had been able to break through the encrypted technology of Jay's phone and get her exact location. Sadie thanked God every day that no one else had been killed.

Val was a trooper, and she was going to recover from her injuries. Sadie hoped to see Val soon. They'd spoken a few times. Val felt that she had failed both her brother and Sadie. Sadie tried to convince her that nothing could be further from the truth, but she knew that Val just needed time to come to terms with all that had happened.

By the time she and Kip got back to El Paso, they

were both ready to be done with hospitals. He'd been referred to a doctor there for his follow-ups. And she was looking for some quality time to talk to him about everything.

She was in love with him. There was no doubt in her mind. But she wasn't sure if Kip would be able to move forward with her given all that had happened. He seemed receptive, but she knew better than anyone that feelings were hard to control.

She'd prayed a lot about Igor and her family—both the family she thought was her biological family, and then the Vladimir family. And of course her adoptive parents who she still relied upon and would always hold such a special place in her heart.

Artur had stayed in touch. She didn't know how to have a relationship with him, but he said he wanted to try. Wanted to start fresh. He was fully cooperating with the DEA and working to put a complete stop to all of Igor's businesses. She had been surprised to find out that Artur had actually put a stop to any of his own illegal businesses the previous year. He'd had to keep up appearances to ensure that Igor wasn't on to him.

Sadie and Kip sat in his living room. Colby hadn't left Kip's side since Kip had returned. Sadie had only gone home to sleep. She wanted to be there to take care of him. He was probably getting tired of her fussing over him, but she couldn't help it.

It was finally time to have the talk. He was well enough, and she'd had enough time to put all of her thoughts together after the roller coaster of emotions.

Sitting next to him on the sofa, she grabbed his hand. "Let's talk."

"I'm all ears."

"First, I'm sorry for not telling you who I really was. I can say I was doing it to stick with the Witness Protection protocol, but that wouldn't be true, considering that I clearly broke the protocol when I decided to go after Igor. I also could say that I wasn't using you. But in the beginning, I was."

"Sadie," he started.

"No. Please let me finish."

He nodded and squeezed her hand.

"Somewhere along the way, though. I got to know the real you. And believe it or not, you got to know the real me. And," she paused and took a deep breath. "I fell in love with you. Completely and totally. I know there are a million reasons why we could never work…"

"Shh." He put his fingertips up to her lips. "Sadie, I've got something to say, too. When I first found out about your past that you had kept from me, I was angry—very angry. I tried to lump you in with the others who had hurt and betrayed me before. But once I got past that selfish reaction, I realized how strong of a relationship we had built over such a short time. You led me back to the most important thing in my life—my faith. You were and are a true partner in every sense of the word. Sadie, I love you."

She couldn't believe it. He loved her! After knowing everything, her entire complicated and sordid past, he still loved her.

She threw her arms around him without thinking, and he grunted.

"Sorry, I forgot about your injury."

"I'm okay." He smiled and ran his hand through her hair.

Colby barked his approval.

"Sadie, you know I told you I love you. And I mean it. With all my heart and all my soul. You drive me to be a better man, and a better servant to the Lord."

She grinned, and her heart bloomed full of love.

Kip knelt down on one knee. "Sadie, will you make me the happiest man alive? Will you marry me?"

She took in a breath. She couldn't believe this was happening. Looking down into his blue eyes, she could feel his love for her. Their relationship had grown from partnership to friendship to something so much more.

"Kip, yes. I'll marry you. I love you so much."

"I love you, too." Kip stood and pulled her up from her chair. Then he leaned down and kissed her softly.

The kiss ended, and she looked into the eyes of the man she loved. Knowing that he was her true partner, now and always.

* * * * *

Dear Reader,

Thank you so much for reading my first book for Love Inspired Suspense. I really do believe that I was inspired to write this story. It may be difficult to imagine finding inspiration through grief, but that's exactly what happened to me. I wrote the majority of this book in the dark days right after my father's passing. In the midst of my grief, I found a certain measure of peace. By writing this story, I found comfort and a reminder of those things my father held dear: faith, love and family. With faith being at the top of the list.

So this book was more than just a story for me. It was a journey to healing, and one I'm profoundly glad that you are now taking with me. While the struggles that Sadie and Kip faced were quite different than what I was going through, writing their story gave me strength and an outlet to work through my pain. Day by day—word by word—prayer by prayer.

Again, thank you for reading *Out of Hiding*. I would love to hear from you! You can visit my website at www.racheldylan.com, or email me at racheldylanauthor@gmail.com.

Rachel Dylan

Questions for Discussion

1. Sadie found faith through the upbringing and teaching of her adoptive parents after her biological parents were murdered. What role did your parents play in your faith journey?

2. Sadie recognized that she was walking a fine line in her feelings of revenge toward Igor. Have you ever wanted to seek revenge on someone, and how did you cope with those feelings?

3. Kip had a hard time dealing with the betrayal of his best friend, Brad. Why do you think he was ultimately able to forgive him? Has there been a time when you thought you would never be able to forgive but then you did?

4. Sadie never pushed her faith on Kip, but led by example. How important is it to lead by example in your everyday life?

5. Artur's story is one of redemption. What does redemption mean to you?

6. Even though Igor and Artur were brothers, they made very different choices in their lives. What do you think of Artur's decision to work with the DEA and take personal responsibility for his actions?

7. Sadly, human trafficking is a very real problem both in the U.S. and abroad. There was no way

that Sadie and Kip were going to leave the othe girls behind in Mexico. What can we, as individu als, do about problems like this that impact peopl on a global scale?

8. Sadie and Kip are both animal lovers. Zoe playe a huge role in locating Sadie. While our own ani mals may not be trained K-9 dogs like Zoe, wha are your pets' special attributes?

9. When Kip found out about Sadie's true identity, h felt an enormous amount of betrayal. How have yo been able to cope with betrayal in your life? Wha role did your faith play?

10. Do you think it was right for Sadie to keep her tru identity hidden from Kip?

11. Even given what happened between them, whe Kip called Brad to help in the search for Sadie Brad didn't hesitate. He owned up to his mistake and was there for his friend. What do you thin makes a true friend?

12. One of the ways Kip found his way back to th Lord was through his grief and struggles over wh he witnessed in Iraq. While our struggles may no be on the battlefield, what trials have you had i your life that have brought you closer to God?

13. Mrs. Newton judged Ms. Milton for working s much and the decisions she made in how to rais her daughter. Sadie was very uncomfortable wit

those judgments, especially since Ms. Milton was doing the best she could for her family. When was the last time you wrongfully judged someone? When was the last time that you were wrongfully judged?

14. What role did faith play in Sadie and Kip falling in love?

15. Do you think Sadie will ever be able to forgive Igor for what he did? Sadie always assumed that her father Mr. Mars was the one who had a connection to Igor, but it was her mother. What do you think Sadie feels toward her mother and father?

COMING NEXT MONTH FROM
Love Inspired® Suspense

Available September 2, 2014

DANGER AT THE BORDER
Northern Border Patrol • by Terri Reed
When biologist Dr. Tessa Clearly teams up with U.S. Border Patrol agent Jeff Steele to combat a rampant toxin at its source, they soon learn someone will stop at nothing to cov their own tracks—even if it means committing murder.

WILDERNESS TARGET • by Sharon Dunn
When her ex-boss wants her dead, Clarissa Jones flees to Montana. Trapped in the mountains with danger closing in, Clarissa's biggest challenge may be trusting survival expert Ezra Jefferson to keep her alive.

DESPERATE MEASURES • by Christy Barritt
Framed for murder, Samantha Rogers escapes to the quiet island of Smuggler's Cove. She doesn't want to trust new b John Wagner, but when danger follows her to the small tow her life depends on it.

SUNKEN TREASURE • by Katy Lee
Rachelle Thibodaux's rescue of a treasure-hunting diver in distress could spell the end for her if they can't find the sun ship full of gold before the pirates who are after it do.

STAR WITNESS • by Lisa Phillips
Witness protection promised a new life for Mackenzie Wint or so she thought. With a compromised cover and a drug c after her, Mackenzie hopes Delta Force soldier Aaron Hann will protect her, without jeopardizing both of their lives.

RANCHER UNDER FIRE • by Vickie McDonough
Frantic to track down his kidnapped daughter, rancher Jackson Durant will do anything to find her, even turn to reporter Mariah Reyes, the one person who could expose his secrets.
